Thumbprint My

SIGN OF THE
BEAST

BY

RICHARD FORREST

D0889527

CB

CONTEMPORARY BOOKS

a division of NTC/CONTEMPORARY PUBLISHING GROUP
Lincolnwood, Illinois USA

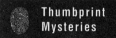

Thumbprint
Mysteries

MORE THUMBPRINT MYSTERIES

by Richard Forrest:

Sign of Blood
Sign of Terror

This is a work of fiction. The characters, incidents, and dialogues are products of the author's imagination and are not to be construed as real. Any resemblance to actual events or persons, living or dead, is entirely coincidental.

Cover Design: Troy Thomas

ISBN: 0-8092-0676-5

Published by Contemporary Books,
a division of NTC/Contemporary Publishing Group, Inc.,
4255 West Touhy Avenue,
Lincolnwood (Chicago), Illinois 60646-1975 U.S.A.
© 1998 Richard Forrest
Manufactured in the United States of America.

1 2 3 4 5 QWM 09 08 07 06 05

CHAPTER 1

"A bear killed him!"

"You think so?" Police Chief Ray Wilson asked. The six foot, three hundred pound chief was not happy. He hated death, and he hated murder most of all.

"It was a bear," Tim Roar said again. The black-haired young police officer was thin and wiry. Behind the chief's back he would often mimic Ray's heavy walk.

They were looking at a dead man on the floor of a one-room cabin. The old man wore overalls and work boots and had white hair and a beard. The arms of his shirt were ripped. Long cuts covered his arms and face, causing him to die from blood loss.

A heavy snow the day before had kept them away from the lonely cabin. When their snowmobiles finally got through, they had found the window shutters closed. They had pounded on the locked door without an answer. Finally they were forced to smash it in. The

1

door now hung from one hinge.

Ray Wilson saw that the windows were locked from the inside.

"Look at those wounds. I know bear marks when I see them," Tim said. "How long do you think he's been dead, Chief?"

Ray knelt by the body that had begun to stiffen. "The doctor will tell us more," he said. "I think he died soon after the snowstorm stopped. What I want to know is, how did the animal get in here?"

"Got me," Tim said.

"The doors and windows were locked from the inside," Ray said.

Tim said, "Look at the size of that fireplace. The chimney's large enough for a bear to have fallen down into the room. Yeah, that's the way it happened. The bear was on the roof and fell down the chimney to find himself facing Old Man Hardy."

"Check the roof," Ray said. Tim went outside only to come back a few minutes later. "Well?"

"I don't understand it, Chief. The cabin roof is covered with snow and there's not a track in it."

"How did the killer get inside?" the chief asked. "And when you answer that, tell me how he got out again."

They had come to the lonely cabin because of phone calls from the old man's daughter who lived in New York City. She was deeply worried because her father wasn't answering his phone. She was afraid for his safety because of the large amount of money he was recently paid for selling some land. Everyone in town knew Hardy kept his money hidden somewhere near this cabin.

Their first look into the room told them why the phone hadn't been answered. There had been a fight that wrecked the inside of the cabin. The table was overturned. A chair was broken in half. The phone wire had been pulled from the wall as the old man fought for his life.

"I want Diff James here," Ray Wilson said.

"Are you nuts?" Tim said. "That retard is only good for sweeping or pumping gas."

"Diff knows animals and the woods. I want his opinion on what happened here."

Tim shook his head. "How do you get an opinion from a guy who can't talk?"

"Did you hear me?"

"Is that an order, Chief?"

"It is. Get Diff. Now!"

*　　*　　*

Diff James slowly carved a small piece of wood he held in his hand. His knife seemed to have a life of its own as he molded the small wooden rabbit. He was a tall, slender man with wide shoulders and a broad smile.

He looked across the table at the pretty redheaded woman who sat across from him. Sun fell through the window and played along her hair. You have hair of red gold, he wanted to say, but couldn't.

A month ago, Ray Wilson had asked his daughter Holly to teach Diff sign language. Holly was a teacher at the nearby school for the deaf. She smiled at Diff as she worked her fingers quickly from one sign to another. "This is cat," she said.

He opened the pad he always carried and wrote the message, 'Signing is for the deaf. I hear fine.'

"You can't speak, which makes you a mute," Holly said. "I know you can hear. Learning this will help you talk with others who sign. Someday it might help you learn to talk. Now, it's your turn, are you ready to try?" She had a smile that really turned him on.

Officer Tim Roar stood in the door of the small garage apartment. "Hey, Dummy. Drop the toy you're making now because the Chief wants you."

Diff stood up with clenched fists and took a step before Holly put a hand on his arm. "No," she said. "He's not worth it."

"Cat got your tongue?" Tim said with a laugh.

"That's not funny," Holly said. "Why does Dad want Diff?"

"A bear wasted Old Man Hardy in his cabin. The Chief seems to think Diff knows bears. Now me, I'd say bears can speak better than Retard here. But I just follow orders." He put his arm around Holly. "Listen, baby, dump the dummy. You and me can have a good time."

"Drop dead!" Holly said.

Diff stepped toward Tim again as Holly pushed between them. "You hit him and you'll lose your job," she said. "You hit a cop and you go to jail."

Diff scowled and wrote on his pad, 'Let's go.'

*   *   *

Ray met Diff and Holly at the door of the cabin. "I need your help."

Diff stepped inside to look at the body.

"I know bear claws when I see them," Tim said.

Diff shook his head and wrote 'no' on his pad.

"Why not?" Ray asked.

"Are you going to believe a dummy?" Tim said.

'Bears don't attack that way,' Diff wrote. 'Those marks look like they were made by someone hitting the old man with a bear claw.'

"This guy can't even talk. How can he figure that out?" Tim said.

Diff wrote another note on his pad. 'Bears sleep a lot in the winter.'

"I have a simple answer to that," Tim said. "The bear was asleep in the cabin. Old Man Hardy came in without seeing him and locked the door. That woke the bear who then attacked him."

Diff wrote another note. 'How did he get out?'

"You know, Chief," Tim said, "I can't very well argue with a guy who can't talk!"

Ray Wilson turned in anger. "We think Diff grew up in the woods because he really knows animals."

Diff took Holly's hand and led her outside to the front of the cabin. The air was clear and bright while a few clouds were white spots in the blue sky. The limbs of large pine trees that surrounded the small clearing were topped with snow. The heavy snowfall in the Adirondack Mountains in upper New York State had lasted for two days. In the distance they could see low mountains through an opening in the forest.

Diff looked at the log cabin's slanted roof. It was covered with more than a foot of unbroken snow. He bent to look at the small animal tracks which were the only marks in the snow. Tiny forked bird tracks, rabbit tracks, and the tracks of another small animal circled the cabin. He bent to examine those marks more closely and decided they had been made by a fox who was probably after the rabbit.

The other marks in the snow were made by snowmobile skis. Footprints led from those machines to the cabin. He knew the first set had been made by Ray and Tim while the later ones were his and Holly's.

'No bear tracks,' he wrote on the pad. Holly nodded in agreement. He wrote again. 'No people tracks either.'

Ray Wilson looked out the door at Diff and remembered the morning ten years ago when he had found him. Morgan, New York, had been deserted at five in the morning when Diff had wandered into town. He had walked barefooted and dazed down the center of Main Street. A taxi had stopped to help, and the driver tried to talk to the young man. Diff didn't answer and began to run down the middle of the street. He stumbled and nearly fell as if very tired. The cabby, worried about the strange young man, used his radio to call for the police.

Ray Wilson had been a captain then and on duty that morning. He was the first officer on the scene and used his patrol car to block Diff's path. When Diff turned to run, he grabbed his arm. He quickly realized that the young man was hungry. They had driven to a diner where Diff had eaten a double order of eggs and ham. Ray did not think it was odd that the man was so hungry. The strange part was that he ate it all with his fingers. He knew how to use a knife, but he acted like he had never seen a fork.

Ray realized Diff was mute when he tried to talk to him but the only response was a series of grunts. After the huge breakfast Diff had fallen asleep at the table. Ray had driven to his house and put the mysterious young man in the bed of the small apartment over the garage. Ten years later Diff still lived over the garage.

Special tutors from school had taught this strange man to read and write. Ray and Holly worked on teaching table manners, wearing shoes, and other things. He learned a great deal, but he still could not talk. Finally Holly had given him the name Diff.

During the next few years while Diff learned, Ray continued to try to find out who he was. He was never able to find where this man had come from. When he asked Diff to write about his past, they found out that he could not remember. He knew about woods, animals, and carving. He knew of little else before the day he arrived in Morgan.

Ray Wilson found Diff a job working for the police department. Diff mopped floors, shoveled snow in the winter, and cut grass in the summer. He also put gas and oil in the police cars.

Now Diff sat on a tree stump at the dead man's cabin. Holly put her hand on his shoulder, and he turned until their eyes met. She smiled. He wasn't sure what he should do. He knew he wanted her, and she seemed to like him. Perhaps she was only being friendly. He turned away to look at the woods and wonder how the old man could have been killed.

Holly liked this strange man and wondered how he felt about her. "How come some of the trees are dead?" she asked. "The pines look all right, but some of the other kinds are just bare trunks."

Diff flipped open his pad and wrote, 'Gypsy moths start white oak blight. Pines don't get it.'

Diff and Holly went back inside the cabin.

"Well?" Ray asked.

Diff shook his head and wrote on his pad. 'No bear or human tracks near the cabin.'

"That's what I thought," Ray replied. "The daughter said her dad sold a lot of land last week. We know the old man didn't trust banks. We've searched the place and can't find a penny."

Diff wrote a longer note on his pad, 'Some men keep their money hidden in a metal box.'

"Maybe," Ray said. "He could have buried it anywhere so we'll never find it."

'Try the fireplace,' Diff wrote. 'Some hide things behind the rocks.'

"How would a retard know that?" Tim asked.

Diff didn't answer. He walked over to the huge stone fireplace and ran his fingers over the rough rocks. After a few minutes he found a loose one at the far end. He removed it to open a hole. He reached inside and took out a metal box which he handed to Ray.

"Empty," Ray said as he looked inside.

"That doesn't mean a thing," Tim said. "Maybe the money wasn't ever there. Big Tom is the bear that did this. I say we form a bear hunt and get the killer."

"We did have trouble with Big Tom last summer," Ray said.

"Sure did, Chief," Tim said. "Campers who kept food in their car trunks had their doors ripped off and the back seats ripped up by Big Tom. That bear is a legend—a bad news animal."

Diff wrote another note. 'Bears don't need money,' it said.

"Maybe retards do," Tim said as he took handcuffs from his belt. "How come you knew where to find the money box?"

"How come?" Ray asked. He put a hand on Tim's arm to keep him away from Diff.

"I think the dummy needs to be leaned on," Tim said. "He knows more than he's telling."

"How can you say that?" Holly yelled.

Diff took her hand and smiled.

"Look at him, Chief!" Tim said. "He's smiling. He knows something. I say we lock him up."

CHAPTER 2

"What do you say, Chief?" Tim Roar said. "How about I take this guy to the station and lean on him?"

"You just try," Holly snapped.

"Retard here knows something, and I want that information," Tim said.

"He knows that some people hide money behind rocks," Ray said. "Knock it off and take another look outside."

"I can't understand why you listen to a guy who mops our floors," Tim said. He gave Diff a dirty look before he went out the door.

Holly and Diff spread a blanket over the dead man. Ray Wilson searched the cabin one more time. It was not a large room, and it didn't take long before he looked over at Diff and shook his head. "A dead man in a locked cabin makes me wonder."

Diff wrote on his pad and tore off the page which he handed to Holly. He followed this with another page which he also gave to her. A puzzled Holly looked at the writing. "Diff says it's not a bear," she finally said. "Not only are the claw marks wrong, but look at this place. A large bear would have finished him off quickly. Old Man Hardy fought like hell with a man, not a bear."

"Bull!" Tim said from the doorway. "I've lived in these mountains all my life and I know a bear killing when I see it! Besides, look at the food cabinet. Big Tom will do anything for food."

"All right, knock it off!" Ray said. "Did you find anything outside, Tim?"

"No, Chief, it's the same out there as it was before. There aren't any other footprints near the cabin other than ours. I also climbed up on the roof to make sure the snow on top is unmarked."

They heard the whine of snowmobile engines and walked out of the cabin to stand in front. As the engine sounds got closer Tim said, "Who the hell is that way out here?"

"Probably city people out for a joy ride," the Chief said.

"They're running wide open," Holly said. "That's a dangerous thing to do around here unless you know the area. There are lots of holes and rocks under the snow that can cause an accident."

Diff wrote a quick message on his pad which he handed to the Chief.

"Bearcats are powerful machines," Ray read.

They watched two large red snowmobiles speed out of the woods and make a wide circle around the cabin. The two men driving the powerful machines wore heavy leather jackets and cowboy hats.

"Yahoo!" They yelled and waved their hats in the air as they made another circle around the cabin near the four people standing by the door.

"Hey, Retard!" one of the men yelled at Diff. "Let's hear talky, talky, talk!" They laughed and quickly stopped their machines with a skidding turn. A blanket of snow spray flew over the four people.

"Watch it!" Chief Wilson said.

"I should have known it would be the Laman brothers," Holly said.

"My favorite guys," the Chief added.

"I thought you told me they were prison bait, Daddy," Holly said.

"I did and they still are. One day I'm going to catch them at something I can make stick. All right!" the police officer yelled. "What are you two up to out here?"

"Just taking a ride in the woods, Chief," Luke Laman said. "Anything wrong with that?"

"Where did you get those machines?" the Chief asked. "I've never seen you ride them before. They look brand new."

"Bought them this morning," Luke said. "No crime in that."

"I'll decide that," the Chief said. "You tell me where you got those machines so I can check that they aren't stolen."

Luke Laman reached inside his jacket and pulled out a crumpled piece of paper. "I can do better than that and show you our receipt. We paid good cash money for these babies."

Chief Wilson examined the paper carefully before handing it back to Luke. "That's a lot of money. Where did you two get that much? The last I knew you two weren't even working," the Chief pressed.

"We just sold five acres of Christmas trees, Chief," Luke said. "We've got good cash money and we're not breaking any law. So it's time you got off our backs."

"Watch how you talk to the Chief," Tim said. "Hey, you two guys are pretty good hunters, aren't you?"

"The best," Joe Laman said. "No one gets more deer in these parts than the Laman brothers."

'Mostly illegal,' Diff wrote on his pad.

"How's that?" Holly said softly.

'Jacklighting,' Diff wrote.

Holly nodded because she knew what that meant. *Jacklighting* was hunting deer at night with a powerful lantern. The light pointed at a deer made them stop still and stare. After that, it was like shooting fish in a barrel and no sport at all.

Luke Laman grabbed the last of Diff's pages from Holly's hand and read the two notes. "What is he putting down here? Who says we jacklight to shoot illegal deer?"

Diff pointed to himself.

"Why, you dummy! I ought to tear you apart." Luke grabbed Diff's jacket.

"Leave him alone, Luke!" Chief Wilson said as he pulled them apart.

"Get your hands off me, Chief. I done nothing."

"I don't believe that. You two haven't worked in two years. Somehow you bought new snowmobiles, gas for your truck, and all the beer you guys drink."

"I told you, we took Christmas trees to the city and made a heap. You can't prove a damn thing so leave us alone."

"Someday I will get you, Luke," the Chief said. "One of these days I'm going to catch you in the act and send you both away."

"You and what army, Chief? Hey, what's going on here?" The brothers saw the broken door for the first time and looked inside the cabin. "Man, that looks like a body under the blanket."

"It is," Ray said.

"Isn't this Old Man Hardy's place?" Luke said.

"You know it is, " Tim said. "A large bear killed the old man."

"No kidding?" Joe Laman said.

"Clawed him to death," Tim went on.

"So that's why you asked us about our hunting? You want to form a hunt to get the bear?"

"I think it's Big Tom," Tim said. "He's the meanest bear in these parts."

"I had him in my gun sights once, but he got away," Luke said.

The Chief examined the new snowmobiles again. "How many trees did you guys say you sold?" he asked.

"Five acres like I said, Chief."

"How come I never saw any trees like that on your land?" Ray said.

"We been working rented land way out of town," Joe Laman said.

"I believe that like a hole in the head," Ray said under his breath.

"I heard that and it's too bad, Chief," Joe said. "You got nothing on us so we're going, we're history. We're open any time for a bear hunt, Tim. Specially if it's Big Tom.

Give us a call and bag up a case of beer." The two men jumped on their snowmobiles. They turned sharply and threw up more snow that slapped against the cabin wall. As they weaved in and out of the trees, they were soon out of sight.

"You shouldn't be so hard on those guys, Chief." Tim said. "The Laman brothers are just a couple of good old boys."

"Let me tell you something, Tim," Chief Wilson answered. "Those guys were stealing toy cars by the age of four. By the third grade they were taking other kids' bikes. I caught them driving their first stolen car at fourteen. Before they dropped out of high school, they tried to steal a train. They got off that time. They still have never done time, but they will one day. Right now, I want to know where they got the cash for those machines. I want more info about their tree sell story. It all makes me wonder about the money missing from the dead man's hidden box."

"We don't know for sure that there ever was any money in that box, Chief. And for all we know maybe the Lamans did sell those trees," Tim said.

"The dead man's daughter said her father sold land last week so he might have had a great deal of cash," the Chief said. "And now we find a hidden box that's empty. Then these two good old boys just happen to ride out here on machines they can't pay for."

"I still think a bear did it," Tim said. "And in that case the only bear big enough to do that is Big Tom. I'll bet he killed the old man in the cabin and ran off to where he hides on Bald Mountain. He's asleep in one of those caves up there right now."

Diff wrote in his pad and handed the sheet to Chief Wilson.

"Bald Mountain is state land," Wilson read. "No hunting there."

"Butt out, Diff," Tim said. "If that's a man-killing bear, we can hunt him down anywhere."

'Then there will be two victims,' Diff wrote in his pad. He remembered a summer three years ago when he had last seen the large beast.

On that warm day, the Chief had dropped him off at the base of Bald Mountain. He carried a small pack high on his back. His few supplies, along with good fishing, would be enough to last him for the week he would spend alone in the woods.

The forest rangers had asked Diff to use a week of his vacation to explore the river that formed in the foothills of the mountain and ran down to Lake Walpie. He was to find out if the eagles had returned to the hills. Diff's love of animals and knowledge of the woods made him a natural for this type of work.

Years ago there had been many eagles here, but they had died when the river fish were poisoned with polluted water. As the great birds swooped from the sky to catch and eat the fish, they too became sick and either died or did not have chicks. For decades the great eagles had been gone from this area. Now that the water was cleaner, they were said to be returning.

As the Chief waved and drove off, Diff began an easy trot that would carry him over the low hills at a mile-eating pace. It was what he called an Indian run. It was the steady pace that for hundreds of years Native Americans had used in their great hunts for deer and other wild game. Diff was a fisherman and not a hunter, but he liked the pace and feel of this run.

His arms and legs moved with the steady, smooth beat of the trained runner. His morning runs around Morgan paid off when he tried to do distances like this. Sun came through the treetops and touched his face. He followed an easy trail that led around the higher foothills until it met the river.

Since he traveled with little food and other supplies, he would have to use all his knowledge to catch fish and find shelter. He did not carry a tent, but he had a light sleeping bag rolled and tied to the top of his pack. If he was caught in heavy rains, he would have to find or build some type of shelter. Otherwise, he would be very uncomfortable.

At night he would build a fire to keep larger animals away from his few supplies. The fire would feel good on the cold mountain nights that arrived even after the warmest summer days.

It did not take long to reach the Jones River that formed from a dozen small streams that ran off the mountain. The river ran many miles from the base of Bald Mountain to lower land where it formed Lake Walpie. The eagles were said to be living along the river banks.

That first night he slept under a rock overhang. The fish were hungry and soon hit the bait on his hand line. He landed a fat bass for dinner. He cleaned the fish with his knife on a flat rock and cooked it in his light frying pan over an open fire. Coffee and dried vegetables completed his meal.

He wrapped up in the sleeping bag, banked the fire so that it would burn low for the night, and soon fell asleep.

A noise awoke him in the middle of the night. It was impossible to tell time in the dim moonlight, but he knew something nearby had moved. The shape on the other side of the fire told him that the visitor was a large animal of some sort.

Diff sat up and pulled out his hunting knife. The low fire cast a glow across the small clearing where he was camped. On the far side of the camp, the large shape moved closer. The beast stood under the tree where Diff had hung his pack to keep it safe from such food attacks. When the beast rose on his hind feet, Diff saw one of the largest bears he had ever seen. With a huge paw it knocked the pack to the ground. Diff held his knife in front of him. If he were attacked by anything that size, he would have little chance to win the fight.

In the dim glow of the campfire he saw the animal rip apart his pack and nose into his supplies. Then the bear looked across the burning coals toward where Diff crouched with his knife.

Man and bear watched each other across the clearing. The bear turned away and slowly disappeared into the woods. 'Thanks a load,' Diff wanted to say. 'I hope you left coffee because I'm going to be eating a lot of wild berries.'

Diff found the first eagle on the following day. The large nest high in a tree was too big for squirrels or other creatures that lived in trees. It had to be an eagle's nest.

He lay in a clearing not far from the tree and watched the area with a small pair of field glasses. Suddenly he saw an eagle swoop down toward the river like a dive bomber. In seconds it was flapping its wings to regain height with a fish in its claws. Rather than landing to tear apart and eat the fish as eagles usually do, it flew up from the river.

The eagle was carrying the fish to the nest. This might mean that there were baby eagles in the nest. The birds had truly returned if they were hatching eggs. He had to find out if this was true.

There was a cliff fifty feet away from the tree that held the nest. If he could reach a good spot on the cliff as high as the nest, he might see the baby birds. The rangers would want to know if there were chicks in the nest.

Diff tied his sleeping bag and the remains of his supplies to a tree branch. Then he began the climb up the cliff. It was a hard climb since the cliff rose nearly straight up from the river bank. At the top he would be nearly level with the eagle's nest and have a good view of the inside.

His fingers curled over the edge of the cliff. He pulled himself up the last few feet and lay breathing hard. After a moment he turned to look toward the tree with the nest.

Again the eagle swooped up from the river. It carried another fish in its claws. If there were no baby eagles in the nest, the bird would have eaten the fish at once. The bird carried the fish to the nest. When the large bird landed on the nest, Diff saw the heads of two small eaglets.

The eagles had not only come back to the river, they were making families. It was a great feeling to be one of the first people in the state to see this. He felt like yelling with joy and might have if he could only speak.

Diff saw movement in the corner of his eye and looked down at the river. There were three of them going toward the river. One large bear and two cubs. He was sure the biggest bear was the one who had raided his camp and stolen the food.

The cubs were small and the larger bear was teaching them to fish. The larger bear stood on a flat rock above the water with a paw ready. The two quiet cubs behind her watched every move.

With a quick move of her paw, the bear flipped a trout out of the water over to the river bank. The fish flopped on the ground as the two cubs crowded around it to watch for a moment before they had their meal.

When she was sure the cubs were eating, the larger animal went back to her fishing.

Diff had seen bears in the woods before, but never one this large. He had heard the stories in Morgan concerning the bear called Big Tom. This had to be the bear that fit that name. It was unusual for a female to reach this size which was what had confused people who had seen her.

There was no question about it, the large bear with the two cubs was Big Tom. However, Big Tom was a she.

*   *   *

Now three years later, Diff remembered the large bear with her two cubs. If it was at all possible, he would never let anything happen to that animal.

CHAPTER 3

Who am I?

He could say the words in his mind, but he could not speak them. Diff James still did not know who he was. His life seemed to start one dawn ten years ago when he walked into the town of Morgan. Before that day his life was a blank slate with no words.

He didn't know why he could not speak. During those first weeks Ray Wilson had taken him to three doctors who did not find any reason why he couldn't speak normally. They tested his intelligence to find that he was not only normal, but a bit above average.

When he came to Morgan, he seemed to know some things and not others. He could read a little and knew a great deal about the woods. There were lots of things he did not know about everyday life that made his days a bit confusing.

When these feelings came over him at night, sleep was

gone and he got out of bed. He had a choice either to read a book or run. He looked out the window of his small apartment to see the first light of dawn come over the hills. The sky to the east was pink, which meant it would soon be light. It was cold out, but the weather was clear so Diff put on sweatpants and shirt. He found his running shoes under the bed and laced them tightly.

He left the small apartment over the garage that was set back from the street. The upstairs bedrooms in the house were dark. Diff knew that Ray Wilson slept in the front bedroom on the second floor. Holly's room was in the rear of the house. She would now be asleep, warm and curled up under the blanket. He wanted to tell her how he felt, but he could not speak.

Diff James began to jog to escape the demons that filled his dreams. He ran to avoid thinking about where he had come from.

The town of Morgan in upstate New York was a small city of ten thousand people whose work depended on tourists. In the summer they took care of campers and fishermen who came for the woods, streams, and clear lakes. Deer hunters arrived in the fall. In winter skiers sped down the slopes, and the woods were filled with cross-country skiers and noisy snowmobiles that scared rabbits and other small animals.

There was little crime in this pleasant town. Ray Wilson's fifteen-man police force spent most of their time on traffic control.

The run cleared Diff's mind as the cold dawn air made him feel better. He liked Morgan and felt it was a good place to live. The area where Ray Wilson had his home was an old neighborhood. Most of the houses had been built near the turn of the century. These homes were large wooden houses with wide front porches. The street went down the hill to Court House Square and Main Street. The small police headquarters was five blocks down Main Street.

Diff could be happy here if a few things were different. If he could speak. If he could have Holly. If he could be a police officer. So many ifs, none of which seemed possible. Without a voice, he could not make the first moves toward Holly, and he could not join the police force.

He wondered if he would spend the rest of his life sweeping floors without a normal life. Was there somehow hope for him somewhere? These questions made him run faster to chase the ghosts from his mind.

He ran to police headquarters where he showered and changed into work clothes. It would be a good morning to begin an early wax of the main floor. Later today he could ask Holly to come with him to check on the land sale that Old Man Hardy had recently made. It would be interesting to know if the dead man did have cash hidden in his cabin.

By eight that morning Diff had a good start on his day's work. When Chief Ray Wilson came into the police station, he saw the shiny floors and smiled. Diff followed his friend into the Chief's office where he wrote on his pad and handed the page across the desk.

'Who am I?' it read. 'Can I look at my file again?'

Ray turned to a file cabinet and took out a folder for Diff.

For the tenth time Diff read the few sheets in the file. They told how Ray Wilson had made a computer search. Ray, then a captain, had contacted New York state police. He had also contacted the New England states for their missing person records. He had hoped that he would turn up a description of Diff with a name. They soon found that there were no records of such a person listed as missing. Ray also checked with mental hospitals and other similar places, but no one like Diff was missing. Wilson had called all the surrounding towns in the area with no good answers.

Where Diff came from was still a mystery. If he had a family, they had not reported him missing to the police. If he had been going through the area, no one had ever asked about him. He seemed to come from nowhere.

Diff went over the file again to see if there were something that was not done. He could not be a police officer because of his handicap. However, he still followed police work closely. He was satisfied that Chief Wilson had tried his best to find out where he had come from.

A medical report said that Diff had memory loss. The doctor thought this was probably due to some sort of accident. His speech loss was before that.

Diff felt that because he had walked into town that morning ten years ago, he had not come from a place more than a few days' walk. The file showed that Chief Wilson had talked to all the towns within a hundred miles of Morgan. Diff knew the town names well for he had spent hours looking at maps of this part of the state to see if any rang a bell with him. He checked off the towns that Wilson had contacted: Royn, Miller, Waycross. The word back from Waycross was like the others, but he had a feeling about that town. He wrote in his pad, 'Ask them in Waycross if anything odd happened about the time I came here.' He handed the page to Ray.

Ray read Diff's note before he took the file back and read it again. "I don't know, Diff, it was ten years ago and people forget."

'Try again,' Diff wrote on his pad.

"Okay. I will. But don't expect much. A lot has happened since you walked into town. For one thing, the local police chief over there has retired and often records get lost."

'Please try,' Diff wrote.

*   *   *

Because he had started so early, Diff finished his work at the station by two. Holly parked her small car in front and honked. He ran out and jumped into the seat next to her. She smiled at him before she put the car in gear.

"Where to?" she asked.

'Lawyer Martin's office,' he wrote on his pad.

She turned the corner toward the Iron Building next to the courthouse. Most of the town's lawyers had offices there. "He's the one who did the land deal for the dead man?"

Diff nodded.

Tad Martin, attorney-at-law, was not just fat. He was so round that his stomach could hardly fit behind the large desk. His body, his face, and his cheeks were round. He looked at Diff and Holly with a dark look that said he was not a jolly fat man.

"I was Hardy's lawyer," he said. "I cannot speak about what Mr. Hardy did or did not do because it is private information." He closed his hands over a very round stomach and chewed his cigar.

Diff wrote on his pad and ripped the page off in anger. Holly read, "Old Man Hardy is dead. We need to know if he had money in his cabin."

"I will not say," the lawyer said. "Now, I am a very busy man. Please go."

"It was made to look like a bear may have killed him," Holly said. "But his hidden money box is empty."

The cigar fell to the desk which said that Martin was

shocked. "You found it empty?"

"It was behind a rock in the fireplace," Holly said. "Did he have money last week?"

"I will not say."

"The man is dead and may have been murdered," Holly read what Diff wrote.

The lawyer seemed to change his mind. "Mr. Hardy did sell 500 acres of good land last week. The deal was closed here in this office. He was paid by a check drawn on our bank."

"Did he cash the check?" Holly asked.

A pause and then, "Yes, he did, but of course I made him get a guard to see him home with all that money."

"I see, and that was last week?"

"Yes, on Thursday."

"He was probably killed after the storm," Diff wrote and Holly read.

"That's all that I can say," Martin said. "He did take a great deal of cash with him to the cabin, but if it was not in the box, he may have buried it."

'Ground too hard,' Diff wrote.

*   *   *

"It's Chief Wilson over in Morgan," Ray said into the phone. "How are you, John? Do you like retirement? . . . Yeah, I know. You miss police work. Listen, I need a favor. Remember several years ago when I asked you about a missing person? . . . That's right, a barefoot man came into Morgan who couldn't talk and didn't know who he was. . . . Yes, I remember what you said. You had no missing persons in your town like him. What I need to know is, did anything odd happen a day or so before my call? . . . Ring me back if you think of anything."

It was three hours later when John White called back. Ray listened for a minute. "You say a pickup went into the river after the driver had a heart attack, and you found *what* on the floor of the truck?" He gripped the phone. "You found a carved wood rabbit? . . . Thanks, John. I would like to see that piece of wood if you can find it. . . . You gave it to your grandson? . . . See if you can get it, would you?"

Ray Wilson hung up the phone and knew there was a slim chance they might be on to something.

*   *   *

Diff and Holly left the Iron Building and walked a block to her car. "Time for another sign lesson," she said.

Diff nodded happily. He didn't care so much for the lesson as he did about being with Holly. 'Fine,' he wrote on his pad.

Holly backed out of the parking place to find their way blocked by a crowd that nearly filled Court House Square. Diff got out of the car and looked over the heads of the crowd to see what was going on. Holly stood by his side and put her hand on his arm.

Luke Laman was standing in the bed of a bright red pickup that was parked at the center of the square, yelling at the crowd. "Your wife and kids will not be safe!" he shouted. "A killer bear is loose and must be killed! Old Man Hardy was clawed to death in his cabin."

There were shouts from the crowd.

"We have to hunt him down," Joe Laman said as he climbed to the bed of the truck next to his brother.

"He must be killed!" Luke added.

"We think he's in a cave up on Bald Mountain, and we need help to find him," Joe Laman said. "Can I have a dozen good men with rifles to go with me?"

There were shouts of the crowd and then yells of "Yes, me!" "I will help!" "I will too!"

"We're going to kill us a bear!" Luke Laman shouted. "A good bear is a dead bear!"

More shouts from the crowd.

Diff wanted to yell, "No! You are wrong!" But he could not talk.

Holly tightened her grip on his arm.

CHAPTER 4

"We all know what did this," Luke said. "Big Tom is the worst bear that ever lived in these hills."

"No man can kill Big Tom," a man yelled. "When my daddy was young, he saw Big Tom. Tom has been here since the land was made. Even the Indians had stories about him."

"You think he's a ghost?" Luke shouted as he held up his rifle. "Let's see how he does after I fire a couple of these babies into his hide."

There were shouts of approval from the crowd.

"Wait a minute, Luke," a man yelled. "The bears are asleep for the winter."

Diff shook his head. The man who made the statement was Henry Watson, who worked in the bank.

"Bears don't sleep all the time," Luke yelled.

"Sometimes they leave the den for food, except for this bear who goes out to kill people."

"I heard Old Man Hardy was killed inside his cabin," Henry said.

"You're no hunter, Henry," Luke yelled back. "If you were, you'd know that Hardy lived in a log cabin and bears can climb. Any bear worth his salt could climb to the roof, but it would take a smart one to know how to get in that way and go for food."

Diff wrote on his pad and gave the note to Holly. 'And get out with no tracks?'

The crowd began to get angry as more men and women arrived in pickups which held snowmobiles and rifles.

Henry wanted to know, "How are you going to find one bear in a whole forest?"

"We all know Big Tom has been seen many times on Bald Mountain," Luke said.

"There are lots of bear caves up there," someone yelled back.

"That's why we need your help," Luke answered. "We'll all go up the mountain and go in all of those caves."

Diff and Holly saw that the angry crowd wanted blood and because of that the hunt had taken on a killing life of its own.

All of a sudden, Chief Wilson was there. He climbed up on the truck bed and shoved Luke aside. "Hold on!" he said in his deep voice that carried across the square. "I want everyone to go home because there will be no bear hunt on state land. With all you people running around up there with rifles, someone will get hurt."

"Let Luke finish, Chief," a man yelled.

"Luke is done!" Ray shot back.

There were many cries of "No!"

"Go home!" Ray Wilson ordered. When no one moved, Ray knew he couldn't move the crowd. He couldn't do it himself and he needed help. He left the pickup bed and went to his car to radio for backup help.

Trucks and cars began to go out of town to Bald Road. They would drive up the mountain as far as the clear road would take them. Then they would switch to their snowmobiles for the final trip to the caves.

Diff wrote in his pad and handed the page to Holly. 'This has got to stop before they kill every bear on the mountain.'

"I know, Diff, but if Dad couldn't stop them, how can you?"

Diff didn't know, but he had to try.

"Back to the house?" Holly asked. When Diff nodded, she took the back streets to avoid the cars going to Bald Mountain. "You know, the people on this hunt are not real hunters," Holly said. "These are the men who hang out in bars and don't care what they kill, even each other. Daddy tried to stop them. Before these people are done, they will kill every animal on Bald Mountain and maybe some of each other."

Diff did not own a snowmobile, but he still had to stop this hunt. For his plan to work he had to reach the west face of Bald Mountain before the Laman brothers. The caves on the west face were the largest, so he knew that's where Big Tom would sleep. Once they reached the end of the mountain road, the way to the caves would be a hard climb through deep snow.

He wrote on his pad, 'Need cross-country skis and snowshoes.'

"I know you have them at your apartment, so I'll go as fast as I can," Holly replied.

Diff thought about bears. There were two kinds of bears, black bears in this part of the country and brown bears in the far West. The blacks weren't as big as the brown bears, such as the Kodiak in Alaska or the mean grizzly. However, a black bear could grow to six feet and weigh over 300 pounds.

Big Tom was one of the largest blacks Diff had ever heard of—more than six feet tall and more than 300 pounds. She was a massive beast—so large that one swipe of her paw could kill a man.

Bears were loners that slept most of the winter, but they did not sleep all day. They would often leave the den during a mild winter day and walk around for an hour or more. In addition to their size, they could swim, climb, and run as fast as twenty-five miles an hour.

Diff also knew that bears were mean, and the meanest was Big Tom. When the hunters found Tom and could not kill her right away, some of them would die.

It was a dangerous time.

Holly braked the car in front of Diff's apartment. He ran inside and went through his closet until he found his snowshoes and a pack. He tucked the shoes into the pack along with water, matches, bread, and meat. He also took a warm hat, gloves, and ski mask. He got the short cross-country skis and poles from the small back porch, and he wore the ski boots. It was going to be a long afternoon.

When they drove past the road to Bald Mountain, two pickups were already there. One man was checking his snowmobile while another was putting shells into his rifle.

"Where do you want me to leave you?" Holly asked. "You won't be able to go faster than those machines."

'I know,' Diff wrote on his pad. 'Going up the west face.'

Holly nodded and turned down Route Nine that went around the base of Bald Mountain. It did not pass the west face, but it was the closest road to that side of the mountain.

Diff opened the door as she pulled the car to the side of the road. He put the pack and skis on. "If the bear is on this side of the mountain you might get to him first," Holly said. "Then what do you do?"

Diff shrugged because he had only a dim idea of what he would do.

"Good luck, Diff. Be careful," she said as she put her hand on his arm. "Be real careful, please."

He nodded and started off over the snow. Cross-country skis are made to go over level land. He moved with the back-and-forth movement of the cross-country skier. He went across flat places at a good clip, and when the land dipped, he was able to pick up speed. As the foothills turned into the base of the mountain, the way became harder.

Diff stopped at a rock that stuck above the snow. He took off the skis and took the snowshoes from his pack. The climb was getting too difficult for the skis and the snowshoes would make better time. He tied the skis and poles across the top of the pack and started off again.

The many hours he spent on his early morning runs were now a help. He was in good condition. With luck he would reach the caves before the others. The machines that came to the west face would have to go on the small road that ran around the mountain.

*   *   *

After a mile of hard walking Diff came to a ranger cabin. The cabin was below the tree line and held spades, axes, and other items for use in a forest fire. Diff used his knife to undo the screws at the lock and was soon able to pry the lock and open the door. Once inside he opened the small window that was high up on the wall. He left the cabin door open and continued up the mountain to find Big Tom.

Even with his morning runs, going up a mountain in deep snow was hard work. After another half mile Diff was nearly out of breath and still hadn't reached a cave.

Then he saw the first cave behind a pine tree. He had walked these hills every summer since he had been in Morgan and knew the land well. He wondered if Tim Roar was with the hunters. Tim, as head of the Mountain Rescue Team, knew this mountain as well as Diff and would think of the west face also.

Diff slipped out of his pack and lined up the skis so that he could put them on quickly after he went into the first cave.

The cave was empty, but droppings told him that animals had lived here last year. When he went into the third cave, he heard the sounds of a great bear's snore and snowmobile engines. The hunters were coming and would be here soon.

Diff saw the great bear everyone wrongly called Big Tom asleep at the far end of the cave. Near her were two cubs, curled up asleep. A glance told Diff they were sleeping on what looked like a canvas bag. Big Tom had been busy at someone's camp again.

The mother bear made a loud grunt and turned over. Diff picked up a rock with the thought, 'Hey, you in the fur coat! Here's one!' He threw the rock at the bear's head.

The great bear turned over with a snort but did not wake up. The sound of snowmobile engines was louder.

The hunters were getting closer and seemed to be on their way to this cave.

In order to wake up the big animal, he was going to have to move a lot closer and throw a larger rock. He might not make it to the cave entrance when an angry bear came after him.

The snowmobiles were nearby. There was little time left. He had another idea. He hated to do it, but it might save the bears' lives.

Diff twisted the ear of the nearest bear cub. The cub gave a yowl that was almost like a dog's yip.

The mother bear was instantly awake and charging after Diff. The only way he was able to make the cave entrance was because the large bear stopped a moment to give the cubs a cuff to keep them back in the cave. When her babies were safe, she started after Diff again.

Diff ran from the cave followed by a very angry mother bear. He stumbled down the hill to the skis, clipped them on, and started the downhill run. A quick look back showed that the bear was right behind him, and the snowmobiles were not far behind Big Tom.

That was one angry bear and she was coming fast!

"There he is!" someone yelled from a snowmobile.

"Can't get a clear shot!" another said.

"You go on his right! I'll go to his left! We'll box him."

"He's after someone on skis!"

Diff knew that the bear was right behind him. He could not outrun the bear, but skis on a downhill run were faster than a man could run. If he could only stay ahead of the animal until he got to the cabin. He hoped no hunter would be able to get a clear shot.

The bear was gaining on him and the men were closing on the bear. It was going to be close. The bear was getting nearer because cross-country skis were not made for fast downhill runs. They were fast enough to keep him a little ahead of the bear, but not for long. The cabin with its open door was in front of him.

Diff skied into the cabin, kicked off the skis, and dove for the small window. The bear went in the door after him. Diff ran around the cabin, slammed the door shut, and closed it with a long board. There was a lot of noise from inside the cabin. That was one angry animal!

"Retard's got him cornered!" Luke yelled as he stopped his machine. He jumped off into nearly waist-deep snow with his rifle held over his head. Other hunters were also near the cabin.

"We can shoot right through the door and get him," Luke said.

Diff shook his head and stepped in front of the door to spread his arms and legs. They could not shoot at the door without hitting him.

"Get away from there, Dummy!" Joe Laman said. "You move or I'll put one right into you."

Diff shook his head.

"There's four of us and one of him!" Luke yelled. "Hit him upside his head with your rifle. Then we can get our bear."

Another snowmobile stopped. Ray Wilson pushed through the snow to the cabin. He carried a pump shotgun in his hands and jacked a shell into the chamber. "Everyone go home," he said. "You hear me? I say this hunt is over!"

"We can shoot you too," Luke said.

"You do and you get a full load from my gun in your gut," Ray Wilson said. "You want it, Luke?"

The crowd began to start their machines and leave.

Ray turned to Diff. "When we're sure they're gone, you get on my Snowcat with me. Then we'll let the bear out and hope he goes home to a new cave. Good work, Diff."

CHAPTER 5

The door to Diff's apartment was not locked. When Ray Wilson went inside, he heard Diff turn over in bed. He went to look at the sleeping man. He sat in a chair by the bed and took a small wooden rabbit from his pocket. He ran his hand over the smooth wood.

"I have come to think of you as my own son," the police chief said in a low voice. "Those early years when you first arrived in Morgan were like raising a small child. You had so much to learn. You are bright, Diff, I hope you know that. No matter what scum like the Laman brothers say, you are smarter than a lot of people." He put the small rabbit on the table and sat looking at it.

"If you could only talk, I would be very proud to have you serve on the force with me. What happened to you, Diff? What did they do to make you mute?"

Diff turned over.

"You did a very brave thing yesterday, son," Ray said. "You risked your life twice. The first time was when you trapped the bear in the cabin. He might have killed you when you skied down the hill. The second was when the Laman brothers might have shot you. You risked your life for an animal, which is a very brave thing."

Diff's eyes opened, and he saw the carved rabbit on the table. He sat up to take the carving in his hands. He ran his fingers over the wood before he looked at Ray.

"John White, the retired chief over in Waycross, found it and called me back. So I drove over there earlier today to get it."

Diff put the carving back on the table and reached for the pad. 'I made this,' he wrote. 'I know my own work.'

"That's what I thought as soon as I saw it. John found it in a truck under water and gave it to his grandson. It was still at the bottom of his old toy box."

'What does he know about me?' Diff put down on the pad as fast as he could write.

"I think you might be from Waycross. A few days before you arrived in Morgan, a driver had a heart attack in Waycross and went off the road. When they pulled the pickup from the water, they found this carving inside."

'I know I carved it,' Diff wrote.

"I want you and Holly to drive over to Waycross and find out about this," Ray Wilson said. Diff was in the shower before Ray had finished.

*   *   *

Retired Police Chief John White lived in a neat trailer with a low white fence. Holly had phoned ahead, and the door opened as soon as they parked. White was a large man with a big head covered with snow-white hair. "Well, just don't stand there like statues. Come on in and we'll have coffee."

Diff handed him the carved rabbit.

"My friend would like to know how you found this and what you might know about him," Holly said.

"What's the matter with him, can't he speak for himself?"

Diff knew from living with Ray Wilson all these years that police officers sometimes spoke sharply. After thirty years of police work, this retired cop's talk sounded like he was giving someone a speeding ticket.

"He can't speak," Holly replied. "But he can hear fine, and he can write on his pad. Do you know who he is?"

"Never saw him before, but come on in and we'll talk anyway." They went into the small living-dining room and sat at the table while John White served coffee. As they drank, White held up the rabbit. "Yep, I found this in the seat of a 1980 Ford pickup. Bill Dawkins had a heart attack and drove into the river."

Diff pointed to himself.

"There wasn't anyone else in the truck when we got it out. There was a rumor that Dawkins had something strange out on his farm. For years he wouldn't let anyone near the place, so no one ever saw anything for sure. From time to time there were stories that folks saw a naked boy running through the woods. They only saw him at a distance, mind you. I didn't pay much mind to it, but the stories kept going around."

"What about a Mrs. Dawkins?" Holly asked.

"She died more than fifteen years ago."

"Could this man Diff be her child?"

"I don't know. Don't he remember?"

Diff shook his head.

"Seems to me there might have been a child out there at one time. I think he died. Yep, I think Dawkins drove into town and told me his little one had died. Hate to tell you this, but Dawkins was a mean one. I don't think that your friend wants that man for a father. He was strange and kept to himself a lot. Some say he believed in devils and the such. Can't your friend remember any of that?"

"He can't remember anything," Holly said. "Perhaps if he saw the house and farm where he might have grown up . . . ?"

"No harm in looking," White said. "The Dawkins place is still vacant because land is cheap around here and not many are buying. The place is falling in and you won't need a key to get in. Here, let me draw you a map of how to get there."

*   *   *

Holly stopped the car in front of the house. The porch was falling down and many windows were broken. The front lawn grass was so high that its ends pushed out of the snow. The barn had missing boards and its door was half off.

"Are you sure you want to do this?" Holly asked.

Diff nodded and left the car to walk up the porch steps and open the creaking front door. He stepped inside to find himself in a small living room. An old sofa with bare springs was along one wall. A large easy chair had a rat's nest in the seat. The faded rug was covered with animal droppings. Leaves, brush, and snow blew in through a broken window.

Diff walked slowly through the room, felt nothing, and remembered nothing. He left the living room to walk into a small dining room. Then he walked back to the kitchen which ran along the rear of the house.

The kitchen sink was stained black. A wooden table was covered with dirty tin plates and cups. A shelf still held a few cans of beans and lunch meat. Some cans had been opened and heated over an open fire built in the middle of the floor. This seemed to show that some kids or some of the homeless had stayed here.

Diff sat at the table while Holly stood in the doorway. She looked at him with worry as he tried to remember sitting at this table and eating a meal. Had he eaten a cookie or a sandwich here? He had no memory of it.

He slowly walked to the stairs. The wood planks creaked as he went up to the second floor. There were two small bedrooms and a larger one. The beds were bare and stained from the roof leaks as the building slowly rotted away. It would not be long before a wall fell and the house began to cave in.

Diff walked through the rooms, trying to remember a young boy who might have slept in one of them. Again, there was no memory.

Holly came partway up the stairs. "Can you remember anything?" she asked.

He shook his head.

"I'll bet you never lived here," she added.

'Not in these rooms,' he wrote on his pad.

She turned on the stairs, and he followed her down into the kitchen. They walked outside by the back door. Diff looked at the distant woods and felt something. He always felt a closeness with the woods, so this place might not be any different.

They walked through the rear yard and could see the tops of rusting machinery poking through the snow. The barn was empty except for a bit of straw here and there. At the rear of the barn was a six foot wide hole in the ground. Diff knew that in the old days ice was often kept under barns. Large slabs of ice were cut from a lake or pond and lowered into a cool room below the ground. The ice would then be covered with bales of straw. The ice would stay frozen through the summer and pieces could be chipped off for use in an icebox.

He stared down into the black hole. A rope hung down from a loft beam and trailed into the black hole. He began to feel something that was a little bit like fear.

"What is it?" Holly asked.

'Don't know, but I have a feeling there is something down there I must see,' he wrote on his pad. 'I have to find out what it is.'

"I can't see a thing in there," Holly said. "Let me get the light from the car." She ran back to the car while Diff looked into the hole. For the first time since they had come here, the feel of fear began to grow.

Holly returned in a few minutes with the flashlight and handed it to Diff. He switched it on and pointed the light into the opening in the barn floor. He bent over to see better as he swept the light back and forth.

"What do you see?" Holly asked.

Diff shrugged. He grasped the rope that hung down from the loft and gave it several tugs. It seemed to be in good shape and able to hold his weight.

"It's not safe to go down there," Holly said.

'Have to,' Diff wrote on his pad. He put the flashlight in his back pocket. Then he took the rope with both hands and swung out over empty space. He slowly began to lower himself into the hole. Ten feet below the barn floor, his feet touched the ground. He let go of the rope, took the light from his pocket, and turned it on.

He slowly turned in a circle to let the light follow his moves. The space under the barn was ten feet on each side. There were bales of straw that proved that this had been an icehouse at one time.

He walked over to something in the far corner. On top of two bales of hay was a pile of old army blankets made into a crude bed. It looked as if it might have been where someone slept. He carefully went over the rest of the room.

There was a large mug on an old table with a stool. Next to the mug was a tin plate and spoon. He opened a wooden crate shoved into another corner. Inside were a toy truck, a cap pistol, and a few items of clothing.

He somehow knew what he might find next. He shone the light over the far wall which ran along the rear of the barn. He felt along the wall until he found a board, so painted and dirty that it looked like the wall itself. He pulled the board away to find steps behind it which were cut into the dirt. He knew that at the top of those steps was another board that opened to the outside. If you shoved that one up, you came out near the barn's rear wall.

"Hey, down there," Holly called. "What's going on that makes you so quiet? I'm coming down." Holly lowered herself down the rope until she was by his side. "Find anything down here that—?" She stopped and looked at him with wide eyes. "Oh!"

Diff had tears in his eyes. He had found the place where he had once lived.

CHAPTER 6

Diff was having a bad dream about the man with no face carrying him into the barn. He tried to cry as he was held over the hole in the barn floor, but there was no sound. He tried to fight, but he wasn't strong enough. He was dropped into the black hole and saw the face of death.

He hit the bottom with a thump and was surprised that he didn't seem hurt. It took him a moment to find that he had fallen on a bale of hay at the bottom of the icehouse. He looked up at the man without a face who was looking down at him.

"Daddy," he tried to call to the man in the black suit and wide hat.

"You are of the devil," was all the man said to him before he left the barn.

He was hungry and cold. He curled into a ball and pulled hay over his body for warmth. He didn't know how much time passed until two old army blankets were dropped down the hole in the barn floor. They fell in a pile on the dirt floor of his prison.

Each day other things came down the hole. On the first day a small wood table fell and landed on its side. On the next day a wood stool fell. Later a tin plate, a bowl for water, a spoon, and a candle were thrown down the hole. Food was the last item. He threw himself on the bread and meat. He tore it apart with his fingers as he stuffed it in his mouth.

He must have done something bad, but he couldn't remember what it was. Something had made his father very mad at him. He was being punished for a crime he did not remember.

"Daddy!" He said the word in his dream and that woke him up. He sat up.

A wide-awake Diff remembered how he cried for the man who might be his father. He could see the room under the barn in his mind. He knew he had been there, but he didn't remember why. His face was wet. He felt the fear of the long fall into the black hole.

Sleep was gone, but the questions were still there. He got up from his bed and felt so cold he shivered. He had cried for his father in his dream. But what had he done? What crime called for such terrible punishment?

Only questions and no answers.

He slipped into sneakers and a sweatsuit. It was late at night and far too early to go for a run. He sat at the table and picked up the knife and the wood he was carving. The feel of the knife and wood were comforting. He had carved the rabbit so many times that he hardly needed to look at it. He remembered carving in his prison under the barn.

He looked at the clock on the night table. It was after one. That meant that today was Saturday, and he did not have to go to work at the police station. On most of his days off he would go into the woods. In warm weather he hiked. In snow he skied or snowshoed. His terror of the room under the barn made it hard to face this long day.

He had to do something to keep himself busy. He didn't want to think about that room and his dream. He knew what he would do. He would go out to the dead man's cabin. He would work on the murder case to keep away from the fear of his own past.

*   *   *

Early Saturday morning Holly looked down at Diff's note and smiled. "I don't see why you can't borrow Daddy's snowmobile since he won't be using it today. I can't go with you because I have to teach at the deaf school. Going for a ride in the country?"

Diff nodded.

"I didn't think you liked those machines. You always wrote that they were too noisy for the woods. But since you're going, I'll call the station and let them know you'll be taking out Dad's snowmobile."

Diff packed a lunch and walked down to the station. He tied his snowshoes to the back of the snowmobile. He started the machine and drove into the woods along a shortcut he knew to the dead man's cabin. This woods trail was far shorter than going by road.

The machine made a great deal of noise in the quiet woods. Holly was right, he hated these loud snowmobiles because they scared the animals. They took men with guns deep into the woods which meant that hungry animals were not safe. Diff hated to ride one, but today he was in a hurry and didn't have a choice. He had a lot of work to do.

He felt like a brother to the animals who lived here. He knew that in his past he had spent many hours alone with those who lived in the forest. This made him sorry for the loud noise and their fear of the snowmobile.

He stopped at the edge of the cabin clearing and put on snowshoes. The broken cabin door had been fixed and the building was shut. He wasn't interested in the cabin as much as the woods around it. There had to be a way for someone to get into that room without leaving marks. Whoever was able to do that had killed the old man and had stolen his money. How did the killer do it without leaving a clue?

The cabin sat in the center of a clearing. Tall pine trees were all around it, but none were near enough for branches to hang over the cabin roof. The closest pine was many yards away from the cabin. He did a slow snowshoe walk around the edge of the clearing.

Because of the fight in the cabin, Diff knew that the murderer was probably a strong man, able to kill with bear claws. He did not know how the killer had gotten inside the cabin, but there must be a sign somewhere. All animals and men leave clues when they move through the woods. It was his job to find that sign and where it led.

He stopped for lunch at noon and sat on a rock to feel the warm sun on his face. He ate a sandwich and sucked on snow. He had gone around the edge of the clearing three times looking for something. All that he found was where hungry deer had eaten bark, a nest of rabbits, and an old fox den.

He finished eating and thought about his next move. He would circle the cabin again, this time further out.

When the sun in the sky told him it was three o'clock, he found it. The clue was a narrow ring mark on the base of a pine on the far side of the cabin. He bent down and gently brushed snow aside to look at the small circle. It was a narrow cut in the bark less than an inch wide that went around the lower trunk of the pine.

He shaded his eyes to look across the clearing toward a tall pine on the far side directly across from him. He quickly crossed the clearing to the pine he had picked out.

He couldn't find any mark on that tree's lower trunk. He was about to turn away and go home when he saw a small cut in the trunk about waist high. The mark was so tiny that he had nearly missed it. He looked at it more closely and saw that the hole was the size a large nail might make if it were stuck into the tree. He found a similar mark above the first.

He could tell by the fresh cuts that these marks had been made this winter. They might have been made after the time of the last snowstorm.

What did they mean? He knew that the small spike marks and the circle on the trunk of the tree across the clearing meant something, but what?

Wood chips flew in his face. A bullet had cut through the tree inches above his head. He heard the sound of the shot a little more than a second later. Diff threw himself on the ground. He heard the zing of another bullet as it passed over his head. If he had still been standing, it would have gone through his back. He heard the shot less than two seconds later.

He knew the speed of sound was 700-some feet a second. That meant the shooter was about 1,000 feet away. A shot of over three hundred yards was a hard one to make in the deep woods. He knew by the sound of the rifle that it was a powerful gun such as a 30-30 with a good sight.

Another shot rang out. This one was lower and hit the tree only inches above his head. This was no mistake or accident. Someone was trying to kill him. He was an easy target with no way to escape.

The killer might work his way closer until he had a sure shot from a few yards away. Metal jacket slugs would rip through Diff's body. He would soon be a dead man.

He would not wait in the snow to die. There must be something he could do. The only weapon he had was a penknife. It wouldn't be much help unless the killer came close to him. He didn't think his would-be killer would get that near. What else did he have that might help? He had to outthink his attacker.

The shots came from the far side of the clearing near where his snowmobile was parked. If there were no snow on the ground, he might try running for it. He might run north and weave in and out between the trees. In the spring with leaves on the trees and no snow, he might make it—except there was snow on the ground. The drifts were over his knees and in places up over his waist. That made it impossible to run fast enough. Snowshoes were not meant for fast footraces, much less trying to dodge bullets.

That was his answer. The killer could not see that he wore snowshoes. While he was looking at the spike marks in the tree, they were pressed under the level of the snow. When he threw himself down after the first shot, the snowshoes were pushed under the snow. What was the killer thinking? He probably thought that Diff would panic and run for the snowmobile. Yes, the shooter would hide near Ray's snowmobile. He would wait near it with a good field of fire for a close shot. He would wait until Diff came through the snow and tried to start the machine. When Diff sat on the seat and turned the key, he would be a sitting duck.

Diff would not go near the snowmobile. His only

advantage was that he wore snowshoes, and the killer did not know that. He could not move quickly over the snow. However, he could go cross-country in the opposite direction away from the snowmobile. If he wasn't shot as he tried for it, he might break free.

Diff rolled over to his knees and jumped to his feet. He moved from tree to tree as fast as he could, away from the man with the rifle. Although he expected shots to ring out, the killer didn't bother to fire. He was waiting for the sure shot when Diff came around to the snowmobile.

Diff went to the far side of the clearing before he turned away from the cabin to go due north. This was away from the man who was waiting for him near the snowmobile.

He had gone three miles from the clearing when he heard shots. He looked back as he heard five shots fired. He saw a flash of flame that blew above the trees near the clearing. The killer had gotten angry at the wait and had shot at the snowmobile until the gas tank blew. The killer now knew Diff had gotten away.

Diff would have to make a wide circle to make a safe return to Morgan. It would be a long hike. He looked at the sky to see that the sun was going down. It would soon be dark and he had hours of travel. He would have to use all his skill to keep from getting lost in the dark.

The attempt on his life proved that he had found good clues when he saw the marks on the trees. He knew they were connected with the murder, but he wasn't sure how.

There were a great many things to think about.

CHAPTER 7

Diff and Ray stood on the small hill across from the blackened snowmobile. The gas tank's explosion had burned all the paint from the machine, burned off the seat covers, and ruined the chrome. It sat in the forest like an old wreck.

"The man who shot at you was probably on this hill," Ray said. "He sure did a number on my snowmobile. We won't worry about that because the insurance will pay for it. In the meanwhile we can use the police snowmobile."

Diff pointed to a series of small holes in the snow.

"Some sort of bird track?" Ray asked.

Diff shook his head and kneeled. He reached his hand through one of the holes. His fingers searched beneath the surface until he found what he was looking for. He held it up for Ray to see.

"It's a shell casing from the gun," Ray said. "That could be evidence, so be careful with it. You told me he fired several times at you, and then there was a series of shots when he blew up the snowmobile. That means there are more casings down there. We'll need them as evidence." Ray took a pencil from his inside pocket which he handed to Diff. "Don't touch the next one you find. I want it tested for fingerprints."

Diff began a search that took fifteen minutes before he had a collection of five shell casings. He caught each of them on the tip of the pencil. Then he dropped them into the evidence bag that Ray held open.

"Good work," the police chief said. "I'll send these to the state police lab and see if they can turn up any prints."

Diff wrote a note. 'Let's follow the snowmobile tracks back to the road. Whoever shot at me probably brought his snowmobile in on a truck. We might find another clue.'

"Good thinking, Diff," Ray said. He started the machine as Diff climbed on the rear seat. They drove slowly to follow the ski tracks from the small hill back to the highway. When they reached the highway, they walked along the edge of the plowed road. The snowmobile ski marks ended, and they found where a vehicle had parked. There were clear tire marks in the snow where the driver had pulled off the road.

"I'm going to get equipment from police headquarters to make a cast of these tire marks. I believe they are wide Dunlops. Do you know who uses those tires on their pickup?"

Diff didn't have to write an answer. They both knew that the Laman brothers used that brand of tire, as did many other people.

"While I go back into town," Ray said, "I'm going to leave you to guard these prints. You might need some protection so you had better take the shotgun from my car."

Diff sat on a snowbank by the edge of the road with the shotgun between his knees. The hair on the back of his neck began to rise. Was someone in the woods sighting a rifle at him this very moment? For the second time in his life, he realized how animals felt when men with rifles came after them. It was his turn to be hunted. He somehow knew it was not the first time, but the fog of his memory kept him from remembering the first.

Only careful animals survived hunters. It was time for Diff to take a few safety steps. He went into the woods and lay behind a tree with the shotgun near his shoulder, ready for firing. This gave him a clear view of the road, yet he was protected by the pines.

It took over an hour for Ray to return with the equipment. In another half hour they had a good cast of the tire prints.

It was dark by the time they returned to Morgan. Ray dropped Diff off at the house. "I'm taking the plaster cast of the tire prints and the shells out to the state police lab in Waycross. Take the shotgun with you and stay in my house. Holly knows how to set the alarm system. Stay away from open windows. Don't answer the door unless you know who it is. Someone tried to kill you yesterday. I think they know where you live and will try again."

Diff nodded and wrote on his pad, 'You know that I will take care of Holly.'

"I know you will," Ray said after he read the note and handed Diff the shotgun.

Holly opened the door before he knocked. "I heard what happened to you yesterday," she said. "Get inside fast so we can set the alarm." She closed the door after him with a smile that turned his knees to water. "It's not going to be all bad tonight. I am going to fix you about the best dinner you've ever had. How does a thick steak, home fries, and my best apple pie sound to you?"

As an answer he leaned over to kiss her on the forehead in a brotherly manner. Her face moved under his lips until she stepped back a pace. Their eyes were inches apart. "We're alone in the house, my dear," she said.

He put his hand on her shoulder and felt her slight tremble. His knees were even weaker than they were before. He wanted her so badly, and yet she was so far from him. He could not speak the simple words to tell her how he felt.

Diff stepped away from Holly and wrote on his pad, 'You cook that great dinner. I have to check the house to make sure we are safe.' He looked to make sure the shotgun was fully loaded.

"Maybe I don't want to feel safe!" Holly said with a suggestive laugh as she hurried into the kitchen.

They were washing the dishes after Holly's great meal when they heard Ray's knock. The signal was, as he said it would be, two fast knocks, a pause, and then three more.

Holly opened the door to let Ray come inside. They reset the alarm and then moved into the living room. The drapes were drawn, and the room was lit by a single lamp. Ray sat back in his easy chair and closed his eyes. "I'm afraid I didn't have any luck," he said. "The tire casts don't match the tires on the Laman brothers' pickup. Our clue didn't work, Diff. We're back to square one."

'What about fingerprints on the shell casings we found in the snow?' Diff wrote on his pad.

"Good question," Ray said with a sigh. "The answer is that the casings did not have any prints at all. That's right—nothing. The lab guys think your would-be killer used gloves when he loaded the rifle. He was smart enough not to leave prints on the shells."

That night Diff slept on the downstairs couch. He lay awake and stared at the ceiling for an hour, thinking of Holly asleep in the room above him. He wanted to say so many things to her, but he refused to say them by writing on his pad.

Sleep finally came with its bad dreams. He was in the black hole again and was using the spoon to build steps to freedom. The dirty, hard work took him a long time. He took off his jeans, shirt, and sneakers as they were the only clothes he had. He knew that it had taken him days—maybe weeks—to tunnel to the surface behind the barn.

Time jumped and fear started. He was running naked through the woods. A silver moon cast light through the pines while animals looked at him with wide eyes. Diff knew that he was running from the man with no face. He also knew that he was running from a man with an ax in his hand.

When he looked back, he tripped over a fallen tree trunk. Before he could get to his feet, the man grabbed Diff's long hair and yanked up his head. The raised ax sparkled in the moonlight as it swung near the soft skin of his neck. Then the ax swept down to thunk deep into the log near Diff's head.

The man laughed. "That will teach you to run from me, evil boy. You will suffer more for that."

He was dragged back to the barn and thrown into the black hole where he lay on the ground whimpering. He heard the man with no face shoveling dirt into the secret passage. Diff had spent so long to dig that tunnel. Now he would have to dig it again. He pressed his face into the cool ground as the shovel continued its work.

He heard a metal clink which he thought was the spade hitting a rock. Diff awoke to know that this was not a dream. He slowly stretched under the blanket and again heard the sound that had alerted him. He listened carefully to the voice of the house.

All buildings seem to have night sounds of their own. They creak and groan in various ways that speak with their own voice. Diff had lived in or near this house for ten years and knew its voice well. He was familiar with the noise it made as it settled, the whistle of the wind on a cold winter's night, and the groans of the heating system.

What he had heard was not a familiar sound. Something was so wrong that he reached down to the floor for the shotgun. He pulled the gun toward him as he heard another sound outside.

Someone was in the driveway. This was not the man with no face who chased him in his dreams, this was a very real person.

He slid off the couch with the shotgun cradled in his arms and crept across the rug. He reached the window by the side of the house that faced the driveway. Then he got to his knees and rested the shotgun against the radiator.

Diff peeked around the edge of the drapes. The night was dark without a moon. Fuzzy light from a street lamp down the block spilled into the drive.

There was a dark figure by the garage. Diff watched the shadow slip to the stairs that led up to the garage apartment. The shadow climbed several steps and stopped.

Diff moved the shotgun to the window ledge and curled his finger around the trigger.

The figure on the stairs by his apartment stopped and then threw something through the window near the door. At the sound of breaking glass, the figure on the stairs jumped to the ground, ran around the side of the building, and disappeared into the shadows.

Diff knew what the figure on the stairs had thrown through the window of his apartment. He ducked down behind the radiator as the firebomb in the apartment exploded. Flames began to lick up the walls in the rooms over the garage.

Diff heard noise upstairs as Ray and Holly awoke. Ray began to shout orders into the telephone while yelling at Holly to get down on the floor.

Diff ran to the rear of the house. It took a moment to unlock the door, setting off the house alarm. He ran around the edge of the garage without trying to put out the fire in his apartment. He was after the man who had thrown the firebomb.

It was dark, and the bomber had a good start into the woods at the rear of the lot. The attacker had gotten away again. Only luck and the fact that Ray had made him stay in the house that night had saved Diff's life.

CHAPTER
8

The morning after someone blew up Diff's apartment, Holly saw that her friend's eyes were red, and he seemed ill. He hardly ate breakfast, and he stared off into space. "I know how you must feel," she said. "You could have been killed by that bomb last night."

Diff shook his head and wrote on his pad, 'No, it's more than that. It's the things from my past that are so hard to live with.'

"The only way to get rid of them is to find out what happened to you in Waycross. We'll go over there today."

'Can't,' Diff wrote on his pad. 'Have to work at the station.'

"You've got plenty of days off coming to you, and so do I. Come on, I'll call Chief White for a meeting, and we'll take a picnic." She held his hand. He felt the warmth of her fingers and smiled. Their eyes met for a long moment until they turned away.

*   *   *

Retired Police Chief John White looked at Diff's message and made a face at the couple standing outside his trailer. "Someone is doing what, boy?"

"He is not a boy, Mr. White," Holly said.

"I know that. Course he isn't. Speak up, Diff! You say someone is trying to kill you?"

Holly sighed. "I told you before, sir. Diff is a mute. He can hear okay, but he can't speak. We came to see you to learn more about his background. You told us the last time we were here that the Dawkins child died years ago. We can't seem to find any record of his death."

"Course you can't. Young-un didn't die in Waycross. The family farm is in the county. That's what I told Dawkins when he told me about the child's death."

"I know it was a long time ago," Holly said. "But can you think of any of the details of what Mr. Dawkins told you about the death of the child?"

"Remember like it was yesterday," White said. "You don't forget things that happened the same day this town had its first bank robbery." The old man closed his eyes tightly to see that day years ago when he stood in the street outside the Waycross Bank.

There had been a shootout. An officer on patrol that day had seen the robbery in progress. He had slammed his cruiser into the curb and jumped from the car with his gun in hand. Shots were fired from the bank, and the officer had fallen in the street.

Within minutes White and others had arrived on the scene. A quick firefight followed with many shots fired between the two robbers in the bank and the officers out in front. Police shotguns had won as the robbers fell to the floor critically wounded.

White had just broken open the shotgun to extract spent shells when Dawkins' old truck had rocked to a halt. The farmer had leaned out the window to yell at the police chief.

"I think my young-un's dead, Chief."

White shook his head. "I have a lot of things on my mind right now, Mr. Dawkins."

"Didn't you hear what I just said? My boy is dead!"

"I heard you, Dawkins. I'm sorry, but there's nothing I can do about it right now."

"You are the police so you got to."

"No, sir, I don't have to do anything. You live in the county, out of the city limits. You must report the death to the sheriff over in the county seat. He will arrange for a doctor to come out and see if the boy is dead. That is the law."

"I know dead when I see it."

"I'm telling you the law, Dawkins. Now go see the sheriff. I have a lot to do here as you can see."

White opened his eyes to stare at Holly. "That's how it happened, young lady. You can see why I remember that day so well."

"Did you follow up to see if he really did tell the sheriff of the death?"

"I had other things on my mind at the time," White said.

"There is no death recorded," Holly said.

"Then he didn't report it."

"Where could he bury the body without a report?" Holly asked.

"Right on his land near the other family graves," White said.

Diff wrote in his pad and gave the sheet to White. 'We will dig it up.'

"You can't do that!" White said. "It's against the law to harm a grave."

I must know, Diff thought as he left the trailer.

*   *   *

Diff swung the pickax with all his strength, but it hardly went into the frozen ground. Holly sat in the car with the heater on. Chief White wore a heavy coat and hat as he leaned against a fence. He looked at Diff as the pick fell again and again on the hard soil.

"You're breaking the law, boy," White said.

Diff wanted to yell that he was not a boy, but he didn't want to take the time to write a note and hand it to the old man. He went on working.

"Breaking into a grave without a court order is a crime worth a couple years in jail," White said. Diff kept on digging. "Do you hear that? I swear, no matter what your girl says, I don't think you hear good, boy."

Holly left the car and walked up to the old man. "If Diff is right, there will be no crime."

"I guess we'll just see about that, young lady," White said.

Diff kept on digging. He saw in his fog of memory another time when he had tunneled out of the barn with the spoon. It had taken weeks to reach the open where he could run at night. A young boy's fears had made him return to the place under the barn when moonlight faded into dawn. As he grew older, he had stayed out longer and longer while he learned to feel for the animals in the woods. Something had always made him return to the place he called home.

On his last night there the man with no face, holding his chest in pain, forced him into the truck. The man groaned as he said, "We both will go this night." He drove faster and faster until they reached the bridge where he turned the wheel and drove off into the water.

The pickax bounced off something hard. Holly and White rushed to the side of the small grave and looked into the hole.

"What is it, Diff?" Holly asked.

Diff gently brushed dirt away from the top of the small coffin. He lifted it from the hole and put it alongside the shallow grave.

"My last warning," White said. "You will be arrested for opening a grave. You lift that lid, and you face hard time in the state pen."

Diff ignored the remarks and used the edge of the pick to break the coffin's lid. He tore the pieces away with his fingers to reveal the inside.

"Oh!" Holly put her hand to her mouth.

"I'll be damned," White said.

Diff turned the coffin upside down.

"Empty!" Holly said. "See," she said to White, "there is no crime since this is not a grave."

"It would seem so," White said. "I think it's time to see Aunt Jane."

"Who's that?" Holly asked.

"Aunt Jane is at the school."

"A teacher?"

"More than that. Aunt Jane *is* the school."

*   *   *

Aunt Jane screamed when Diff walked into the Waycross School. She held a test paper in her hands and looked up at him with fear. Aunt Jane was an older woman who wore large glasses. Her hair was pulled back in a tight bun. She looked shocked. Her hand flew to her mouth as she screamed again.

Holly brushed past Diff to take the teacher's arm. "He won't hurt you. None of us are here to do you harm."

"He's dead!" were the first words Aunt Jane said. "He's a grown man now, but I know my kids. He is young Billie Dawkins who died years ago."

Diff wrote a note which he gave to the frightened woman. 'You know who I am?'

"Of course I do," Aunt Jane said. "I always know all my kids no matter how much they grow. I knew you from first and second grade, Billie Dawkins."

Holly found a coffeemaker in the corner and made them each a cup. Aunt Jane stood while her comfortable desk chair was taken over by the retired chief. White leaned back in the chair with his coffee cup. "Aunt Jane is called Aunt Jane by everyone in the parts," he said. "And that's because for the past thirty years she's been teacher to just about everyone around here. This isn't just the Waycross School, this is Aunt Jane's school."

Aunt Jane gave a snort. She was a no-nonsense sort of person who did not take nice words easily. "Never had children of my own," she said, "so I remember each child that comes to this school. I remember you well, Billie Dawkins. Well, what's wrong with you? Aren't you going to tell me where you've been all these years since you aren't a ghost?"

"He can't speak," Holly said.

"What does that mean?" Aunt Jane asked. "Why can't he talk?"

"We don't know," Holly answered.

The teacher looked at Diff. "Well, Billie, how are you

going to tell me where you've been all these years?"

Diff bent over his pad and began to write a long note. He looked over at Holly before he crossed out what he had written. In its place he wrote, 'You tell her.'

"It started one morning ten years ago," Holly began. "Diff came to the town of Morgan and . . ."

When she finished, Aunt Jane faced them with tears in her eyes. "Mr. Dawkins had a funeral service for Billie. Did you know that?"

"No, we didn't," Holly said.

"It was at the graves out on the farm. Mr. Dawkins preached wild things that didn't make much sense. And all that time, the boy was hidden under the barn!"

"Yes, it would seem that he was," Holly said.

Aunt Jane pushed Chief White out of her desk chair so she could pull a file from the drawer. She showed it to Diff and Holly. "Here are Billie's early school records," she said. "Look at his picture. You can see it's him."

"Yes, it is," Holly said.

Diff wrote a note on his pad. 'Where is my mother?'

"She's dead," Aunt Jane said. "Your mother died before your father said you died. I visited her in the hospital at the time. Your daddy took her loss badly. I think that might have been what set him off."

It was Diff's turn to turn away and look out the window. Now he had lost a mother he never knew.

Holly put her hand on his arm. "It's time to go, Diff. There is no more to learn here."

*   *   *

The highway from Waycross went down a very steep hill before it came to the town of Morgan. In order to keep the cost down, the road had been built straight down the hill. A sign at the top told drivers of the steep hill and told trucks to shift to a low gear. Diff did not pay attention to the sign.

"Aren't you going too fast for this hill?" Holly said in a voice filled with fear.

That got his attention because she was right. He was going far too fast for the road. Diff eased off on the gas pedal and gently braked.

His brake foot went to the floor. He pumped it again and again, but his foot kept going right to the floor mat. Without brake pressure the car began to pick up speed.

"Diff, I'm scared," Holly said.

He nodded to show that he heard. His foot kept pumping the brakes, but the car didn't slow down. Holly looked down at his foot and knew what was wrong. "The brake is gone?"

He reached for the emergency brake and yanked it all the way toward him. The car seemed to slow for a moment and then began to speed again. The emergency brake was not strong enough to stop them.

Diff knew that something had been done to the brakes. Someone knew they would be going down this long hill. Whoever had done it wanted to kill them.

They sped even faster. "I am really scared," Holly said.

Diff ran the car against the guardrail to bump its speed down, but it didn't work. Each time he ran against the rail, they heard the screech of metal while he almost lost control of the car. Past the guardrail was a drop of two hundred feet. If they went off, they would die.

Holly put her hand on his arm and spoke in a low voice. "We are going to die, so I want you to know that I love you, I have loved you for a long time." Then she shut her eyes and braced for the crash.

CHAPTER
9

In the distance Diff saw a curve that they would never make at this speed. The road went to the right, but the car would go off the cliff. Its speed would carry it a dozen yards across empty space like a cartoon character who does not realize that the cliff has stopped until he sees that he's walking on air. After a few yards, the car's nose would tilt, and they would plunge onto the rocks hundreds of feet below. At this speed there was no hope the car could make that turn.

A sign flashed by so fast that it took a moment for its meaning to sink in: ESCAPE ROUTE FOR RUNAWAY TRUCKS.

Diff knew that the escape route was a ramp going from the road up a steep incline. It was built to stop large semi trucks whose air brakes did not work. It would also work for a runaway car whose brakes were broken.

Here goes nothing, he thought. He drove the car up the escape ramp at one hundred miles an hour. They began to slow as they neared the end of the ramp. At the far end, where the road ended at a large pile of sand, the car slowed to a stop and gently pushed its front end into the sand.

* * *

Ten minutes later a state police car stopped and radioed for a tow truck to take them to a garage in Waycross. An hour after that, Diff and the man on duty had the car up on the rack, looking at the brakes.

"Never saw that before," the mechanic said as he held up a cut brake line. "Looks to me like someone cut this."

Diff knew someone had. 'Just fix it,' he wrote to the mechanic.

* * *

As they drove back to Morgan, Holly sat stiffly against the door without speaking. Diff pulled to the side of the road and stopped to write a note. "Did you say something to me just before the crash?" Holly read aloud. "I didn't hear what you said." Holly looked at him. "It wasn't important," she said in a low voice.

Diff thought that it was very important. She had said she loved him. He didn't know what to do about it, but he was damned if he'd write her a note that said, 'I love you too.' He could not support her or even talk to her. He had no claim to her at all. He felt like half a man. He would never let her know what he had heard.

Diff increased the speed of the car until her hand at her mouth made him slow. "Please," Holly said. "We came close enough to a bad accident already today. Let's not make one on our own."

As they came to the town of Morgan, the road swept up a short hill. At the top of the rise, they could see the town spread before them in a valley. On this side of town the last building in the city limits was the Morgan Bar and Grill. It sat at the base of this hill like a sore on the town's nose. As they drove by, all they could see were dark windows with flashing beer signs and the Laman brothers' red pickup truck parked in front. Instantly, Diff knew that the Lamans were responsible for the firebombing and the cut brake lines.

Diff yanked the steering wheel hard to the right and drove into the lot. He jammed his foot down on the brake so hard the wheels locked and shot gravel up to the bar's front window.

He was filled with rage. Those same brakes had almost killed them two hours ago. The man with no face filled his dreams, and the Laman brothers were like all the forces that kept him from talking to the woman by his side. Diff jumped from the car and ran toward the door.

"Diff, no!" Holly cried as she ran after him. She reached for him, but he broke away from her. "Don't do this. They aren't worth it. You don't know for sure that they cut the brake lines in our car. Let Daddy handle it."

Diff pushed through the bar's front door into the dim room. He heard Holly behind him still calling his name.

It was a nearly empty, dimly lit place. It took a moment for his eyes to adjust from the bright sun to the dark bar. Four Eyes Marlee was working the counter. He looked up at Diff without interest and then went back to reading his sports paper.

The Laman brothers were the bar's only customers. They were at the far end of the room bent over a dinging pinball machine.

"Hey, man!" Joe Laman said. "Look at that sucker go." Diff balled his fists as he walked toward the brothers.

"Look who just crawled in," Luke Laman said when he saw Diff.

"Well, I believe it's Old Retard himself," Joe added.

Four Eyes looked up from his paper and for the first time seemed worried. "Watch it there, Diff," he said. "We don't want no trouble in here."

Diff did not look at the man behind the bar as he walked toward the Laman brothers. These men were all that he hated and feared. They were men with no faces. They were the ones who had tried to kill Holly and him earlier that day.

"Watch it, Retard," Luke said. The brothers seemed to feel Diff's hate and backed up until they were against the pinball machine.

"You try to fool with us, and you will get hurt," Joe Laman said. "Got that?"

Diff aimed the first punch directly at Luke. He felt the blow hit and Luke gave a grunt. They went into a clinch until Joe Laman crashed a bar stool across Diff's back.

"You guys stop that!" the bartender yelled.

Diff spread his arms wide and threw himself forward. He caught both Lamans and all three men slid under the pinball machine.

"All right, you guys, I've had it!" the bartender yelled

Diff felt only a rage that wanted to pound these men into pulp. He had been shot at, his home had been blown up, and these men had tried to kill Holly. Diff pulled his arm back for a hard blow and felt the click of metal around his wrist as he was handcuffed.

Ray Wilson's large hands pulled Diff off the Lamans. He was dragged across the floor while the bartender went over to the Lamans to wave a baseball bat at them.

"Fight's over," Ray Wilson said. "I'm taking you in, Diff."

*   *   *

Ray parked the cruiser behind the police station and unlocked Diff's handcuffs. They left the car and went inside by the back door. Diff knew the way and went down the hall into the holding cell and closed the bars. He sat sadly on the bunk and buried his head in his arms.

Chief Wilson stood outside the cell and banged angrily on the wall. "When are you going to stop letting those Lamans get to you?"

Diff wrote Ray a long note that said, 'Holly and I were in Waycross today and were nearly killed. On the way home the car brakes went out. At the garage I found out they had been fixed to fail. I am sure that the Laman brothers did that.'

Many emotions passed across Ray's face as he read about the near death of his daughter. His lips changed into a thin line while his large hands opened and closed in anger. "Those guys could do something like that. And they just might. Our problem is that we can't prove it. Even if we could, we can't take the law into our own hands." He looked at his friend and pointed an angry finger. "You drove back to Morgan and passed the Laman's truck parked outside the bar. That's when you lost it, isn't it?"

Diff agreed.

"Looks like we have to get someone else to mop our floors," Tim Roar said as he walked up behind Ray to look in the cell. "I heard about the fight at the bar. You going to can him, Chief?"

"I think the worst we can get him on is disturbing the peace," Ray said. "But I don't think the Morgan Bar is going to press charges."

"Still might be better if we got a new man to work here," Tim said. "We can't have our janitor fighting in bars."

"I'll decide that," Ray said as he swung the cell door open. "Come on, Diff. Let's get you out of here." They walked back to the Chief's office while Tim went out on patrol.

"I want to put you someplace to cool off for a couple of days. It will have to be a place where you will be safe. Someone has tried to kill you twice, so it has to be somewhere out of the way, but I don't want you too far away. It can't be at my house because that would be too easy for another firebomb. It has to be someplace that no one would ever suspect."

He took a few moments to think. "I think I know just the spot."

*   *   *

Ray drove the snowmobile with Diff on the rear seat. He turned off the road into the deep woods and went three miles before they stopped. Ray parked the snowmobile in front of the murder cabin with its yellow police crime-scene tape over the door.

He turned to face Diff. "We're here. I know you're mad, Diff, and I can't blame you. God only knows I'm ticked off over what almost happened to you and Holly. But you have to cool it and not attack those guys. I want you to stay out here at Old Man Hardy's cabin until I come for you. We're through with the crime scene and have gone over everything with a fine comb. You'll be safe here. No one in the world, not even Holly, knows where you are."

Diff nodded.

"You must promise me that you'll stay out here until I send for you. If you nod yes, I know I can trust you."

Diff nodded again.

While Ray removed the tape and unlocked the door, Diff grabbed his backpack containing food, books to read, and a warm sleeping bag. They went into the cabin.

"It's chilly in here, so you had better lay a fire first thing," Ray said. "I'm leaving you the shotgun for protection."

'Thanks for the chance,' Diff wrote on his pad.

"Well, I've got to go back to work," Ray said. He paused by the door. "You know, unless we figure out how a man got in here to get Old Man Hardy, we're going to have to mark this up as a bear killing."

Diff shook his head.

"Have it your way," Ray said as he climbed back on the snowmobile. "But I'll need more than a shake of the head. You've got to figure out how someone got inside a locked cabin, killed a man after an awful fight, and then got out again, leaving it locked from the inside." The snowmobile roared to life and sped off.

There was a pile of logs and sticks near the fireplace. Diff put two logs on the fireplace grate with space between them. He piled wadded paper between the logs with small sticks on top of that. When he had a good base, he put on larger logs before he lit a match to start the paper.

In minutes the fire warmed the room. It was soon very pleasant inside the small cabin. Diff took off his jacket and turned to look at the mess left by the fight.

The police had not changed anything. The room was still the scene of a very bad struggle between man and animal, or was it man and man? The table was overturned with its nearby chair broken. The phone had been pulled from the wall. It looked like a war had been fought here. He may have been an older man, but Old Man Hardy was a tough one. Only a man in good shape could put up a fight like the one that took place here.

Diff went around the room putting it back in order. He set the table back on its legs. He found an unbroken chair in a corner and put it by the table. The pieces of broken chair joined the logs in the fire. Diff used an old straw broom from the corner to sweep up broken glass and dishes.

He found what was left of the phone under the bunk bed. There was no way it could have ended up in that spot unless it had been thrown across the room. He picked it up and walked back to the place on the far wall where it came from. The phone wire was still hooked to the receiver but not to the outlet on the wall. It had been yanked violently from the wall with a strong pull. It was the kind of thing a man might do if he wanted to break the phone before it was used. It was not something that could accidentally happen if a large animal was killing someone. It was obvious that a man had made sure the phone would not work.

There were now three items that convinced Diff that this was a murder rather than an animal killing. The claw marks on the body did not seem like they were made by a bear. The broken phone looked like some person did not want a call made. The long fight that took place in this room was between man and man, not that of an older man overrun by a huge bear.

It took Diff another half hour to finish cleaning the room, spread his sleeping bag on the bunk, and put away his food. He lined his books on the fireplace mantle. He had the feeling that he would have plenty of time to read until Ray sent for him.

He sat on a low bench not far from the fire and went over the murder scene again. The wooden shutters had been pulled across the windows and closed with a two-by-four crosspiece. The door had been locked from the inside.

If the killer had been waiting for the old man to return here with the money and then killed him, how had the killer locked the door from the inside when he left?

There had to be another answer, and it would not come from inside the cabin. The clue would be outdoors. It was time to go out to gather more firewood, so it wouldn't hurt to take another look at the land around the cabin.

Diff left the cabin and walked a dozen feet beyond the door. He turned around to look at the cabin and the forest around it.

On the day someone had shot at him he had found strange marks in two pines on either side of the cabin. The only way for a man to get inside the cabin without leaving prints in the snow would be to climb high into one of those pines and jump to the top of the chimney. That was impossible.

Diff waded through the snow to the pine on the far side of the clearing behind the cabin. This was the tree where he had found small marks cut in the trunk. The tree on the opposite side had a small round band cut into its base. He was sure these were important clues.

He jumped for the lowest branch and pulled himself up. It was a hard climb, but he was able to get high enough up the tree until he was above the cabin.

As he climbed, he found more marks cut into the tree's trunk. When he stopped climbing and looked across the clearing, he had a mental flash of something he had seen last year.

When he put together what he saw here and the thing he saw last year, he knew the answer to the mystery.

Now Diff not only knew how the killer had gotten in and out of the cabin, he also had a good idea of who it might have been.

"We want you out!" Joe Laman yelled at Police Chief Ray Wilson. "You have gotten nowhere on this case. Old Man Hardy was killed by a bear, and you won't do a thing about it."

The hall near Ray's office was filled with angry people. The Chief stood in the door to his office with his arms folded. The Laman brothers, one with a bandage over his nose, stood facing him.

As people pressed closer to Ray, Tim took a shotgun from the gun rack. He pumped a shell into it and stood next to his chief. "Leave!" Tim ordered.

No one moved.

"Make way!" came a yell from the back of the crowd. "Here comes the mayor."

Mayor Will Randall pushed through the crowd until he stood in front of Ray. The mayor was a tall man with a small face that always looked worried. "You had better give these people what they want, Chief," the mayor said.

"You forget that my job does not depend on votes," Ray said. "I have to uphold the law, and in this case killing animals is against the law."

"I hired you, Ray," the mayor said in a low voice. "That's why I tell you to do what they want."

"I *am* doing my job," Ray said. "If you don't like it, then I quit!" He ripped the badge from his shirt and put it in the mayor's hand. "I've had it."

"So be it. I appoint Tim Roar the new chief," the mayor said. He took the badge and pinned it on Tim's chest. There were yells and clapping from the crowd.

"You don't know what you're doing," Ray said.

"It's time for a new bear hunt," Tim said. "Big Tom won't be safe this time. He will be killed and—"

"We'll have bear steaks tonight!" Luke Laman shouted.

There was a loud sound from down the hall. "What in the hell is he doing?" someone said.

"Who is it?" the mayor yelled.

"That guy who can't talk," Luke said. "Watch out for him."

"Get out of here with that!" Tim said as he waved the shotgun at Diff.

Diff pushed a blackboard past the crowd into the doorway of the Chief's office. He turned it until it faced the group in the hall and then wrote in large chalk letters, 'I know how the old man was killed. I can prove it was not a bear. Follow me to the cabin.'

*   *   *

More than a dozen snowmobiles were pulled into a circle at Old Man Hardy's cabin. Men drank coffee and shivered in the cold.

"Get on with it!" Tim Roar yelled at Diff.

"Better show them soon, or they'll go on their hunt," Ray said. He took the chief's badge back from Tim Roar.

"Be careful, Diff!" Holly yelled.

At the tall pine tree on the far side of the cabin, Diff put spikes on his boots. He had a wire over his shoulder. He put a strap around the tree trunk and held its ends. He worked the strap up the trunk and began to climb.

The spikes dug into the trunk, making a set of small holes like the ones he had found before. He worked the strap above him as he climbed.

When Diff was ten feet above the top of the cabin, he fixed the strap to his belt. This gave him both hands free to work with the wire he took off his shoulder.

He put together the mountain climbing device known as a Tyrolean traverse. This was a thin wire that ran from a tree on one side of the clearing across to a tree on the far side of the cabin. The wire went over the cabin's chimney.

He snapped a metal ring with a wooden handle onto the wire. He swung off the tree while holding to the ring mounted on the wire. He slid down the wire until he stopped over the chimney where he lowered himself down to its rim. He dropped a thin nylon rope down the chimney.

A yell went up from the crowd.

"He's inside!" the mayor said. "And he didn't leave a footprint anywhere!"

Diff then climbed out of the cabin up the rope to the wire slide and slid down the rest of the way to the tree on the far side.

"He did it!" Holly yelled as she hugged her father.

"Arrest the Laman brothers," Ray commanded.

"They're gone," Holly said, "but I think Tim took out after them."

*   *   *

Diff knew a shortcut from the cabin back to town. The wind whipped his face and snow blew across his back as he pushed the Snowcat to its fastest speed. He took risks as he raced over the hills too fast. It was only his knowledge of the country that allowed him to avoid the rocks and deadfalls that he knew filled these woods. He reached the police station without an accident.

The clerk at the front desk seemed to be the only person in the station. "Diff just walked in the door, Chief," the clerk said into her microphone. "Tim's got the prisoners in the holding cells. . . . Yes, sir. Over and out." She looked up at Diff, who stood in front of the desk. "Chief wants you back there with Tim. See that there's no rough stuff."

Diff hurried to the two cells at the rear of the building. Tim Roar stood in front of the cell that held the Laman brothers. He was talking to them in a low voice.

"Here comes Retard," Luke Laman said. "Why don't you throw him in the other cell for the crime of being dumb?"

'What's going on?' Diff wrote on his pad.

"I caught them trying to get out of town," Tim said.

"Break Retard's fingers and he won't be able to talk," Joe Laman said with a laugh.

*   *   *

Ray Wilson and Holly hurried down the hall. The Chief was very happy to see the men in the cell. "Good work, Tim. Take Luke into my office for a little chat."

Tim unlocked the cell door and slapped handcuffs on Luke Laman before he pushed him down the hall toward the chief's office.

"You don't look too worried," Holly said to Joe Laman. "You guys are going for murder."

"Are we now, Missy? Maybe you just better wait and see."

Holly turned to Diff. "You know, no matter what we think of him, Tim always seems to be around when you need him. He's either capturing prisoners or taking messages for Daddy. I guess we really can count on Tim."

'What messages?' Diff wrote on his pad.

"Well, all kinds. Seems like everytime I call here I get Tim on the line. Like the day you wanted to take the snowmobile, Tim took the call."

Diff grabbed Holly's hand and dragged her down the hall. He made a quick note on his pad. 'We must get to Tad Martin, Old Man Hardy's lawyer. Quick!'

*   *   *

Lawyer Martin had not lost any weight since they had seen him last. He also was not any happier to see them. "I told you two that I am a very busy man."

Doing what? Eating? Diff thought.

"I can't give you any more of my time unless you need a lawyer and can pay my fee."

Diff ignored the remark and wrote a note on his pad. 'When we were here before you said you got an escort for Old Man Hardy. You wanted someone to take him and his money to the cabin. Who was that escort?'

"I did what any good lawyer would do. I called for a police escort."

'WHO!!' Diff wrote in capital letters.

"Tim Roar, of course. One of the best cops this town has."

Holly's eyes widened as she looked at Diff. "And Tim is captain of the Mountain Rescue Team."

Diff nodded and wrote a long note on his pad. 'Tim was the one who knew Old Man Hardy had money at the cabin. He was also the only person who knew I would be out at the cabin alone at the time someone shot at me. His work on the rescue team means he knows how to rig a wire like I did today at the cabin. We have one more place to go before we'll have it all put together.'

"I think Daddy is going to need our help." Holly said.

CHAPTER 11

Ray and Tim played good cop, bad cop with Luke Laman. It was Tim's turn to be the bad guy. Tim did not hit Luke, who was handcuffed to a chair, but he looked like he was about to.

"We know you did it," Tim said in Luke's face. "Your rat brother has turned you in. He said you killed the old man when he didn't want to. That means murder one for you, Luke."

"I was in the bar drinking beer that night," Luke said to Ray. "Check it out."

"I will," Ray said as he gave an order over the phone.

Holly and Diff entered the office without knocking. "Out!" the Chief ordered. "This is a police interview."

Holly waved the notes she held in her hand at her father. "Diff wants to ask Luke some questions."

"The last I heard, Diff was the janitor here and not able to ask anything," Tim said.

Holly did not look at him. "We want to know how Luke knew Diff took Dad's snowmobile to the old man's cabin! We want to know how Luke knew since Tim took the call! Someone tried to kill Diff out there that day."

"That's got nothing to—" Tim said.

"Diff wants to know when Luke joined the Mountain Rescue Team and learned how to rig a wire."

"I lead the rescue team and Luke's not on it," Tim said.

"Diff wants to know how Luke knew of Old Man Hardy's money when Tim was the police escort."

Ray looked grim. "I think we need to hear from Tim on these things."

"You going to listen to a damn dummy, Chief?" Tim said in anger.

"Explain this, Tim," Holly said as she took a bear paw with claws from her pocketbook. "We found this in your apartment."

"No! You couldn't!" Tim yelled. "I threw the claw in an ice hole at Loon Lake."

"You are under arrest," Ray Wilson said to Tim. He began to read him his rights from a card he pulled from his back pocket.

"Like hell!" Tim pulled his gun and knocked over the chair holding Luke. He put his arm around Holly's neck and backed toward the door. "You move and the girl gets it. Got that, Chief? You come after me and your kid goes bye-bye!"

Tim pushed Holly down the hall. Ray began giving orders on the phone as soon as they heard a truck race down the drive into the street. "Get me the state police," he said. "Where did you get that bear claw?" he said to Diff.

Diff wrote a note that said, 'We cut the paw off the stuffed bear in front of the Morgan Trading Post.'

"Well, I'll be damned," Ray said.

"Tim paid us for the bear hunt," Luke said from the floor. "He gave us money to buy the snowmobiles and a load of beer. We only did what he paid us to do."

"I told my men and the state police to block all the roads in and out of Morgan," Ray said. "There's no way he can get away."

Diff didn't think any road block would stop a mountain man and a member of the rescue team. Tim would go across the hills and avoid any roadblocks. Diff ran for the door.

*   *   *

Diff knew Ray kept the keys to his truck over the sun visor, and he saw that the Snowcat was still in the back. He didn't think Ray would mind a loan of the truck if he could bring Holly back.

Tim would know that all the roads out of town would be blocked by police cars. It was Diff's guess that he would go over Bald Mountain on a snowmobile.

Diff went by the road at Bald Mountain and looked for Tim's truck. At the end of the road he did a U-turn to go back the way he had come. He had missed something. He had not seen any empty truck. Tim's truck could not go off the road in all that snow. What had he done with it and where was he?

Then he saw it and hit the wheel in anger. At the side of the road was a mound of snow higher than the other

drifts. Tim had driven the truck into the ditch until it
tipped over on its side. He had covered the truck with
snow and driven the snowmobile up the mountain. Diff
saw two sets of footprints near the snowmobile tracks.
Tim still had Holly.

Diff took Ray's snowmobile off the truck and followed
the tracks that Tim had made in the snow. He stopped
near the forest ranger cabin on the crest of the last hill
before Bald Mountain. He could see Tim's snowmobile
near the building. The killer was inside the same cabin
that Diff had used to trap the bear.

The whine of the snowmobile's engine was too loud. If
Diff was to reach the cabin without being seen or heard,
he would have to wade in the drifted snow.

He hid the snowmobile behind pine trees and started
off toward the cabin. It was hard going. He sank up to his
waist with each step and was soon out of breath. He
would have sold his soul for skis and that shotgun, but
there wasn't time to go back for them. There was no
telling how long Tim would stay at this cabin, but it
would probably be until nightfall. Then he could make
his way over the mountain without being seen by a
spotter plane.

When he reached the cabin, Diff quietly climbed up
the slanted roof. His plan was to go across the roof to a
position over the door. When Tim came out, Diff could
drop down and overpower him.

He inched his way across the roof until he was nearly
at the peak over the door. Suddenly the snow on the roof
slid to the ground with a loud rumble. He tried to hold
onto the peak, but the surface was so slick that he
slipped and went off the side into the snow.

"What the hell!" he heard Tim say from inside the cabin.

The door was thrown open and Tim stood looking down at Diff who was flat on his back in a drift. "Well, look what we got here," Tim said. "The dummy isn't so dumb after all since he did manage to find us. Too bad about that." He pointed the gun directly at Diff.

Holly stood behind Tim with her eyes open wide with fright. "Diff!" she managed to say.

"Say good-bye to your boyfriend, pretty lady," Tim said. "Because right now I'm going to give him a couple slugs."

"Are you?" Holly said. She swung a forest ranger fire spade directly at the back of Tim's head.

Tim Roar dropped the gun as he stood in the doorway of the cabin with a very blank look on his face. He slowly fell face down in the snow.

"Shall I hit him again?" Holly asked.

Diff shook his head and began to tie his prisoner.

CHAPTER 12

After Diff and Holly had tied their prisoner with all the rope they could find at the cabin, Diff went to get the snowmobile. It was a tight fit, but the powerful machine was able to move slowly down the mountain with all three of them aboard. They chugged down at a snail's pace toward the highway and Ray's truck.

When they arrived at the truck, Diff and Holly struggled to lift Tim into the truck's cab. Tim still had his handcuffs on his belt, so Diff used them on the prisoner and kept the key in his right pocket. With his legs bound together and his arms handcuffed behind his back, Tim wasn't going anywhere except to jail. Then Diff and Holly climbed into the cab of the truck, side by side.

Tim awoke as Diff started the truck and hurried down the mountain road. Tim groaned as the truck rocked back and forth, banging his head against the passenger door. When he was wide awake, he became very angry.

"Let me out of here! You hear me, you two idiots?" He jerked and twisted, quickly finding that he couldn't move anywhere. Diff and Holly smiled at each other. They were not worried about Tim's escape. There was no way Tim was going to leave the truck until they got him to the station. He could yell as loud as he liked as far as they were concerned.

"I'm warning you, Dummy," he yelled as his head banged against the door again. "Let me go this minute or you'll pay for it the rest of your life."

Holly turned to glare at him. "You're a killer who will probably spend the rest of your life in jail," she said.

"Fat chance. I'm going to hire the best lawyer money can buy. I'll beat this thing yet."

Holly looked surprised, and she worried a bit before she turned to Diff. "You know, he still has the old man's money. He'll be able to hire the best defense lawyer in the state."

"That's tooting for sure," Tim said. "No one saw what happened to the old man, and I'll have witnesses like the Laman brothers who will say a bear killed him. Old Retard here will have to use a pad to give his evidence about the way the killer got into the cabin. How do you think he's going to look in court since he can't speak a word? Cross examination time, hah! The jury will laugh at him." He broke into gales of laughter.

"Well, if they don't get you on the murder charge, there's another one waiting for you that does have a witness. I'm that eyewitness along with several others who saw you kidnap me," Holly said.

Once he thought about that possibility for a minute, the hope went out of Tim's voice as his laugh died. When he spoke again, his tone was softer. "Okay, maybe you have a point. So listen up, Holly. Let's have a little talk about Old

Man Hardy's money. There's a lot of it, which means that you and the dummy could have one hell of a time in Vegas or maybe down in the islands. There's enough for you two to go to anyplace in the world. Maybe you'd like to spend a year or two in Europe or something."

"No way," Holly answered.

"Dump the dummy, forget the trip we took together just now, and you and I could have a great time."

"Don't you ever give up, Tim? You are looking at life without parole. You aren't going anywhere—ever."

Ray was waiting outside the building when they arrived back at police headquarters. He rushed over to the truck as Diff and Holly climbed out. Holly hurried to hug her father.

"I don't know how to thank you, Diff," Ray said. The big, tough police chief had a tear in his eye as he looked at his daughter with a love that had been shaken by her kidnapping.

After she gave him a kiss, he turned his attention to the man left in the truck. "You scumbag!" Ray said to Tim. "You're a disgrace to the force." The Chief opened the passenger door and pulled Tim out. Tim collapsed whimpering into the snow. Sergeant Toms cut the ropes around Tim's legs and rushed him into the building to one of the holding cells.

"We have to find Old Man Hardy's money, Daddy," Holly said. "Tim is going to use it for his legal defense. Isn't that something? He kills a man for the money and then uses the same money to defend himself in the murder trial."

"We've already searched his house," Ray said. "I went over the whole place myself, and there's no money there."

"It could be anywhere," Holly said. "We have to force him to tell us."

For the first time in hours, Ray smiled. "We don't beat up our prisoners anymore, honey," he said. "There's no way I can get that money from Tim unless he tells us where it is or we happen to find it. This is a big country, and he might have hidden it almost anywhere or even given it to a friend in the next town. Hell, even the Laman brothers could have it, but I doubt that Tim would trust those two creeps."

Diff wrote a note that simply said, 'I know where it is.'

Ray read the note twice before he handed it to Holly. He looked at Diff carefully. "You know, I just believe you might know where it is. Let's go talk to our prisoner."

They walked to the rear of the police building where the cells were and stopped in front of the one holding Tim Roar.

Tim came to the door and curled his hands around the bars. "Okay, you guys want to deal?"

"You are garbage," Ray said. "When I called the old man's daughter about his death, she told me why Hardy sold that land. That money was for her child's education. Hardy was trying to educate his only grandchild. He sold that land for love, and you stole the money for greed."

"You're breaking my heart, Chief. Like I said, do you want to deal? Drop the murder charge, and I might remember some interesting things."

"Like where the money is?"

"Mum's the word, Chief. Until you make me a deal."

"You'll rot first!"

Diff remembered the bear hunt and the odd bed the bear cubs slept on. Everything fell into place. He wrote a long note that he handed to Ray.

The chief read it aloud. "'I believe the money is at the Sign of the Beast. Tim hid the money in Big Tom's cave because he knew it would be safe there. When the bear hunt started, he knew he could be first into the cave. He would kill the bear and get the money back. Everyone would think the killer was dead, and he would be safe and rich.' We'll just check that out," Ray said.

"Look at his face," Holly said.

They looked in the cell to see the stunned look on Tim's face. Diff's gamble had paid off. They all knew where the money was hidden.

*   *   *

There was a crowd in Police Chief Ray Wilson's office. The mayor, most of the police force, Diff, and Holly were there. Police Sergeant Ned Toms brought in two bottles of wine which Holly passed around in plastic cups.

Ray raised his cup in a toast. "This is for Diff James, who not only saved my daughter, but solved what was almost a perfect murder."

"Hear, hear!" the mayor said. "To Diff."

The two Wilsons in the office had thoughts they did not speak. Ray wanted to appoint Diff a police sergeant if only his young friend could speak. Holly would always wonder if Diff had heard what she had said in the car that day.

The phone rang. Ray spoke a moment and then handed it to Diff. "Chief White over in Waycross wants to congratulate you on the case."

Diff scribbled a note on his pad and handed the phone to Holly. "This is Holly. . . . Thanks for saying that. We are all proud of Diff. He wants to ask you something." She read the note and said, "Diff would like to know where his father is buried. . . . What? . . . We didn't realize that. Where is he? . . . Thank you, Chief White." She hung up the phone and turned to Diff.

"When John White said your father had a heart attack, he didn't mean he was dead. His heart attack was followed by a stroke. Since then he has been a patient in the Waycross Nursing Home."

Diff slowly put down his cup and left the room. As Holly watched him leave, she knew where he was going and ran after him. "Diff! Wait! Don't do this!"

She arrived in the parking lot as Diff was driving away in a police cruiser. Holly knew that in each police car a shotgun was under the edge of the seat. She ran to her car.

*   *   *

Diff James walked stiffly into the nursing home. He handed the clerk at the desk a note which read, 'Where is Mr. Dawkins?'

"Where he is any day at this time," the clerk said. "In the sunroom at the end of this hall."

Diff nodded thanks and walked down the hall. He felt the weight of the shotgun hidden under his raincoat. He had already jacked a shell into it and flipped off the safety. The gun was ready to shoot. He would wait until he was next to the man with no face before he would fire.

He would kill the man for the days and years of hurt done to a small child. He would shoot the man with no face for the dark prison where he had been kept. He would murder the man with no face for the loss of his voice, his life, his love.

He would fire the first shot directly into the head of the man with no face. The second shot would be into his own body.

Diff entered the sunny room. It was empty except for a wheelchair at the far end that held a man in a blanket.

He let the raincoat slip off and fall to the floor. He raised the shotgun to waist level and gripped it with both hands while one finger curled over the trigger.

He must make certain before he fired. He reached the man in the wheelchair who either did not hear or care that he was there. He lifted the right hand of the man with no face and looked at the name, William Dawkins, on the hospital ID bracelet. It was his father.

Diff slowly turned the wheelchair until the man faced him. He raised the shotgun until it pointed directly into the man's face.

The man's eyes were cloudy. His face was blank. He didn't know that Diff and the gun were only inches away. He seemed to see past Diff with the look of the very old and very ill.

"Don't do it, Diff!" Holly cried from the door. He heard the click of her shoes as she ran across the floor toward him.

The man sitting in front of his shotgun now had a face. It was a face without a man, a look without knowledge. Diff's finger tightened on the trigger.

Holly stopped a few feet away and spoke in a low voice. "It's not worth it. Look at him. That isn't your father. That isn't the man who kept you in that hole. You will be killing a man who is already dead."

Diff flipped the safety on and let the shotgun fall to the floor. He took Holly's hand. They walked away from the sunroom and the nursing home, away from the nightmares that had filled his sleep.